IRELAND LORELEI, CASSANDRA JOY, W.A. ASHES

Reigning on Earth

Phoenix Voices Publishing

First published by Phoenix Voices Publishing 2023

Copyright © 2023 by Ireland Lorelei, Cassandra Joy, W.A. Ashes

All rights reserved. No part of this publication may be reproduced, stored or transmitted in any form or by any means, electronic, mechanical, photocopying, recording, scanning, or otherwise without written permission from the publisher. It is illegal to copy this book, post it to a website, or distribute it by any other means without permission.

This novel is entirely a work of fiction. The names, characters and incidents portrayed in it are the work of the author's imagination. Any resemblance to actual persons, living or dead, events or localities is entirely coincidental.

Ireland Lorelei, Cassandra Joy, W.A. Ashes asserts the moral right to be identified as the author of this work.

Ireland Lorelei, Cassandra Joy, W.A. Ashes has no responsibility for the persistence or accuracy of URLs for external or third-party Internet Websites referred to in this publication and does not guarantee that any content on such Websites is, or will remain, accurate or appropriate.

Designations used by companies to distinguish their products are often claimed as trademarks. All brand names and product names used in this book and on its cover are trade names, service marks, trademarks and registered trademarks of their respective owners. The publishers and the book are not associated with any product or vendor mentioned in this book. None of the companies referenced within the book have endorsed the book.

First edition

This book was professionally typeset on Reedsy. Find out more at reedsy.com

Contents

Finding Happiness	1
Forbidden Love: The Tale of Sarandiel and Adrian	20
The Fall of Fire	41
The Legend of the Phoenix	109

Finding Happiness

Reigning on Earth

FINDING
Happiness

SHORT STORY WRITTEN BY
Brittany Wright and Dakota Cole

Gods and goddesses roam the earth.

Finding Happiness

While roaming, they search for their own worth.
Something so magical, something so free
Unlike their ways, more believed.
Falling in love with the way of the world,
The gods fell in love with the earthling girls
The goddesses fell in love with brute mortal men
And that's where this story begins.

Carina

Holy miracles on a stick! When my twin brother and I arrived on Earth, we had no idea what awaited us. Father told us we had to make amends with earthlings and find a true way to happiness. What amends did we need to make with the earthlings? I didn't hurt the earthlings. Neither did my brother. However, we were both sent to Earth like trash being taken out in the otherworlds. One thing that was fact, my twin brother, Cosmo, and I had much to do before we could prove we were worthy of the Summerlands again.

I'm not a bad goddess. Honestly, If it weren't for Jasper breaking my heart, I wouldn't have demolished the pearly golden gates leading to the perfect land. Without him causing my anger to seep through my pores and erupt through my veins, I wouldn't have forced the elder gods to make the ultimate decision and there would be no redemption for me.

I'm going too fast.

Let me explain.

My arch nemesis, Venus was constantly after Jasper, and Stella always wanted what Venus wanted. They wished they were the original Gemini twins. *Typical.* And I have wanted the amazing Jasper since I was three years old. Jasper was my

Reigning on Earth

betrothed and we were set to wed once we reached our peak maturity. Unfortunately for Jasper, he never matured.

The more we fought to stay together, the more the universe had other plans for us. The world ceased to exist when I walked in on Venus and Jasper having the time of their life. He was supposed to be with me. The feeling of my heart being crushed between my ribs, my voice being stolen, my heart being betrayed. I absolutely fell apart and broke.

Jasper broke Carina. He literally broke me. Which caused me, Carina, to throw Jasper into the Pearly Gates. Because of this outburst, my twin and I were stuck in a punishment for me to find a new meaning and purpose for life. How was that fair?

Jasper broke my heart. I get sent away and lose my home until I find a new form of happiness. Jasper gets to live happily ever after with the slutbucket twins.

Broken. Destroyed. There was nothing left for me to go on for any more.

Arriving on Earth was different from what I initially expected. I figured it would be grim and disgusting, but it wasn't. It wasn't as bright as Summerlands was, but it wasn't as dark and grim as the Underlands. The waters smelled of salt and the trees were absolutely breathtaking. I do not believe it was a coincidence that we arrived on Earth during a sunrise.

Watching the sunrise over the ocean was the most breathtaking sight to date. And I've seen the brightest of colors my entire life.

Cosmo and I walked away from the beach and into the cabin, my father set up for us. It was a beautiful cabin, fully furnished and with an amazing view from all of the windows.

Detailed on the breakfast bar was a list of demands from our father. Starting with our careers and the tool to download all of the knowledge for each career. Cosmo would be an electrician and I would be a nurse at the local hospital. We were in Clearwater, Florida, and staying in a cabin a few miles from Largo Medical Center, where I would work at the ER. *How would anyone be happy working at a hospital and long hours?* I thought to myself wanting to go back to the Summerlands and take a different punishment. This one punishment was the absolute worst.

"Carina, chin up. We just have to find something or someone to make us happy and we will save the world, find ourselves, and go back home to rule Summerlands. We just have to survive the earthlings first." Cosmo was always right and convincing.

"I just don't see how I was the only one to get punished. If Jasper wasn't messing with Venus during our betrothal, none of this would have happened." I took a deep breath because I knew it was going to come out selfish.

"You literally demolished the pearly gates and told everyone in Summerlands to eat a demon dick. What did you expect to happen?" Cosmo, right again.

"I'm not sure, Cos, I just know I wanted so much for Jasper and me to rule Summerlands together. Now, we're stuck on Earth and he still gets to sleep with Venus and Stella. It's totally unfair." I sobbed, "Dad was being extremely unfair!"

I threw my long black hair into a ponytail, needing it not to fall to my waist while getting these uncomfortable scrubs on. I downloaded all of the information about being a nurse and I was able to do my job. Everything happened the same with Cosmo, but instead of nursing information, he received the electrician's information.

"Carina, I love you. You're my twin sister. We're going to get through this. With your blue eyes and long black hair, you're surely able to find someone who loves you for you and find your happiness here." Cosmo went on, reading the rest of Dad's instructions. That week, I started working at the hospital. I worked as a shadow with two different nurses: Daxton and Dana. They weren't twins but were very knowledgeable in their work and that was helpful. Daxton was very smart and delicious to work with. He was six foot two and had the most amazing body under his scrubs, his wide eyes, and plump lips just begged me to kiss him. He was a lot more understanding than Dana was, but also not as strict. Of course, he spent most of his life getting the knowledge and I pressed one button and was a senior-level professor with all things medical. It was fun playing the part and pretending not to know what I was doing.

Cosmo was instantly promoted to one of the head electricians. He instantly fell into a routine with his job and didn't hesitate at all to fit in with his new life. I tried so hard to be like him and find happiness at my job, but it just didn't come naturally. I still missed Jasper. Even though he ruined and shattered any chance of us being together within the next ten millennia, I still wanted Jasper. That was my original plan and I wasn't ready to grow away from it.

Uh…. I want to be so much like Cosmo but no, I am here starting this new job at the hospital sorting out med carts and having to deal with old men hitting on me or old women throwing their shit at the wall. Yeah, you wouldn't believe the shit we have to clean up. There seriously needed to be healthcare reform.

However, there are a few points to the job that make it enjoyable. In a very rare occasion, there are the sweet and rare patience that breaks my heart. An example? Mrs. Jefferson, room 129 on floor four. She has been here at the hospital for about a month now because of cancer. Do you think the lady allows it to change her or even bother her? No, not at all! She has been fighting this whole time and it is the patients like that. That has me thinking that I just might start loving my job as Cosmo does.

I am grabbing something from the nurse's closet like Daxton had asked me to do when I hear a loud bang come from down the hallway. At first, I thought that someone had knocked over something. As I eased the door open though I found that a man had Daxton by the front, his nurse's shirt up against a wall, while yelling at him in his face.

Daxton was no scrawny guy. Absolutely not! He had the body of a demi-god, who was always in a gym on his days off. He had sandy blond hair that hung over his one blue eye and one green eye. He drove me wild. Secretly, I had the biggest crush on him and thought his eyes were the most beautiful. I couldn't get the ovaries to tell him, though. He was a nurse in med school. With him around, it didn't take much for me to feel like a dwarf amongst the giants. Of course, when he asked me out on a date, I didn't tell him no. There wasn't much to keep us apart. We worked every day together. We were on call together and when it happened, we shared the same off days.

When he asked me to go on an official date with him, I melted. Without hesitation, I said yes. We introduced Cosmo to Dana and thought they night hit it off. After our first ten dates, we invited them on a double date with us. With Daxton and me going strong, and knowing Cosmo, I wasn't sure if it was a good idea or not to mix our worlds. For whatever reason, I always felt like my twin was judging me. He wasn't ever happy with how I turned out. I let him down. That has always been how Cosmo has treated me.

Since we were kids, I felt like his shadow. If I didn't do things how he did or follow his lead, I was doing it wrong and a burden. NO matter how much I tried or how hard I pushed, I was never good enough to be his twin. Eventually, it became tiring to always put up with it. I felt like I couldn't be myself. Twins or not, the bond wasn't always there.

* * *

Cosmo

Why couldn't Carina be more like me? I walk into a room and everything stays the same. The second she's at my hips, she draws attention to her like the force she is. I wish for once we could have a day where it's not just about her. We wouldn't be on this godforsaken planet if it wasn't for her! I completely understand why she lost her shit. I do. However, the fact is she put the entire universe at risk when she attacked the pearly gates. The gates had been enforced for centuries and now the Elders are telling my parents, in order to restore order and save the universe, She and I both have to find love and happiness outside of Summerlands. We have to find a purpose away from where we grew up and got our roots.

Jasper absolutely deserved to be thrown into the gates, however, I didn't realize she was that strong. Of all the things for her to do that would put the entire universe at risk, she takes her celestial anger out on a little demi-god who isn't worthy of her love or time. Luckily, she still had her chastity so she would be able to maintain a life outside of Summerlands and gain the respect of another suitor. Hopefully.

Finding Happiness

When we arrived, I loved watching her eyes light up and watching the sun rise over the beach. Dad really did a good job. I still don't understand why I was subjected to this bullshit.

When we reached our cabin, we found our career and a new identity. We were keeping our names, but I'd be an electrician and Carina would be a nurse. An Electrician wasn't much different than a dream weaver, yea?

I was happy to try something new and move on to something that wasn't the Summerlands. I have visited other planets before. Ironically, Earth isn't like the others. Mars was pretty cool, but Earth isn't like that either. It's not as hot. It is not like it was all that great anyways the air was bad in Saturn and the women were so superficial. Always happy to be off that planet in the start of new life and find happiness for the points in my life. But my sister can't really say what she wants other than Jasper.

For what reason? I do not know but that man was horrible. On earth, the women here seem to be more genuine and beautiful, and exotic. It was new, and at this moment, I needed something. With the time I lived my sister, on the other hand, seemed all she wanted was to go back home in the Summerlands..

Because of the stunt Carina pulled, if we did go back we would go back to absolute ruins. By destroying the Golden Gates, the elder gods have decided we aren't worthy to rule. The Gemini Twins would not rule at this time.

Of course, by the time we left there, immortal people were dying off, and getting sick. Within the mind, body, and soul, heaven as Earth knew it was fading away and turning to dust.

I do know that Jasper, the man who my sister loved, did something really stupid and broke her heart. After meeting with our parents and the elders, we agreed she and I would go to a new planet, with the goals of finding purpose, true love, and meaning in life. We agreed to go together because we've never been apart.

When she was told Jasper wasn't being punished and he would stay with the two harlots who betrayed her trust and the sanctity of their relationship, she started moping around.

So when my sister asked me for a double date with a guy she just met at her workplace, I was thrilled to see her doing something other than being at home mopping around Jasper. I wasn't expecting this date to happen so quickly, but Carina has been working long hours at the hospital. If we were true Earthlings, we would be millionaires by the time we finished a year here.

* * *

Carina

Cosmo has done nothing the whole time but he thinks I am still a young naive, virgin girl… Little did he know, I lost my virginity to Jasper a long time ago. Before he made the biggest mistake and fell in bed with two other women, but probably too soon because we were still to be betrothed. My brother doesn't even know the true story of what happened between me and Jasper. He thinks he knows, but ultimately, he has no idea. I let him think he knows everything. Twin or not, he will not take everything from me..

As I said earlier, I made the ultimate mistake. This mistake of throwing Jasper at the pearly gates has put a mark on my wings and now I have to make everything right again. With this

Finding Happiness

new start, I plan to find everything lost to me on Summerlands. With this new happiness, purpose, and beginning, maybe I'll find a way to move on from Jasper and when I return, I can rule with a heart of gold and a soul full of gratitude. That's the goal anyway.

The question that torments me is what if I don't ever want to go back? I know I am a goddess. Ruling the Summerlands is something I was brought up to do. However, I am not sure I will ever be ready to do. Returning to Summerlands means I have to continue with Jasper and I'm not sure if I can ever trust him again. Apparently, I'm the only immortal who believes in monogamy.

"Hey, Cosmo, are you still thinking about going home after this? The reason I ask is that I…" I was rudely interrupted

"No, if and or buts you are going back home and they are going to replace you for having a mate as well." Cosmo fussed.

"They already said Jasper was my betrothed. I don't get another. If I find love here on earth, would I be able to live my life with them? Do I get to tell them I'm a goddess and we're about to go to their equivalent of heaven?" Confused. I had so many questions. He seemed to know things I didn't, but wouldn't share all of the details with me.

* * *

Cosmo

Carina would be good at running Summerlands. She would excel in everything our parents have taught us. It wasn't for me. I had a gypsy soul. Even though I was an immortal god,

I wanted to be more than that. I wished I was given a mortal soul so I could appreciate the world as the earthlings did. Their lives are so fragile, yet they live every day as if it's their last.

The double date with Dana, Daxton, Carina, and I was interesting. Dana was a pretty little nurse. I want to say she was in her late thirties. She had long brown hair, a beautiful physique, and curves for days. Her eyes were a golden hazel and sparkled every time she smiled.

When we arrived at the Japanese restaurant, I didn't know what to expect. Being immortal, we didn't need to eat, but feeding humans was a great gesture and showed you really liked them, or something. Forgive me, I was still learning.

I didn't want to return back to Summerlands. I've lived there for a few millennia already and felt my time on earth could justify another reason for me to stay and monitor the earthlings. And if I found my purpose here, could I really leave her?

"What do you want out of this life?" I asked Dana while Daxton and Carina were all googly eyes with each other.

"I want to live knowing I made a difference and helped all those I could help. Regardless if it's at a hospital or if it's at a grocery store, I want to know that I helped everyone I could." Quite possibly the most perfect answer and it came from a mere human. I now understood why the elder gods sent us to Earth to complete this task.

"What do you want out of this life, Cosmo?" She asked me. A dimple peaked from her smile and it was obvious she was flirting with me.

"I want to find purpose and know I did everything I could do to….your answer was perfect. There is no way I can beat that." We all laughed.

"What do you feel like a good purpose is?" Carina asked

Finding Happiness

finally adding to the conversation.

"I think if you live your life with great morals, help others, and follow your heart and soul with good intentions, that's a good purpose," Daxton said. I think that was the moment Carina fell in love with him.

"Do you feel a single person could be another's reason for living?" I asked.

"I don't know. I don't feel like any one person should take that burden to be the reason another is happy." Dana said.

"I'm not sure I'm qualified to be in this conversation. You're very thoughtful and that was quite possibly the most beautiful answer." I laughed again.

"I think you should have your happiness and purpose before you find your person…" Daxton added staring into my sister's eyes.

"Do you have your happiness and purpose?" Carina asked Daxton.

"I do. I am three weeks away from getting my final degree and I am ultimately happy with my life." Daxton answered.

"Could I be your person?" Carina asked. Daxton pulled his hand away from hers.

"That is very possible. However, we've only known each other for a few weeks. I think time will tell if you're my person and if I am yours."

Carina put her hand back in Daxton's to see if he would pull away from her again and when he didn't I saw the beautiful smile take over her soul.

We planned for a night of bowling and then skating after dinner. We all got up to leave and walked toward the exit. I got up, pulled back Dana's chair, and helped her up. Daxton followed suit with Carina. When she held on to his hands, he gripped hers harder.

Carina pulled me to the side and with the biggest smile said, "I am starting to think that the best place to find happiness is to be with the person they love most in the world, whether it is a guy, girl, or both. Do you think we can find our happiness here?"

"Only time would tell," I said to her, smiling. We ran to catch up to our dates. We had a long night planned.

* * *

Carina

Everything was finally coming together. I felt the reason I was really here was finally known to me. After being hurt, shunned away, and served to sentence my punishment on Earth, I found my heart really wanted to be here.

With all of the talks with Cosmo about our situation, Summerlands and taking over after Father, I found myself over Jasper and falling in love with Jax. If Mates were a thing, Daxton would be my mate. No matter what happens, I feel like I am stuck in my head over the future, so much it's hard for me to let go and open up to Dax. Will I be stuck here? Can I go home? Can Dax come with me? Thoughts torment me so much and so often, I miss half of the conversation.

My brother. My source of strength. I'm not sure I could have survived this sentence without my brother. Looking back on everything that brought us here, I'm glad it happened the way it did.

I needed to change after our long date. I walked to my room

Finding Happiness

to change clothes, glancing into the mirror and seeing my smile. *I'm smiling bigger than the cat that caught the cheese.* I think to myself. This was the happiest I have ever been.

As I walk back out to the room, I see Dana and Dax talking and cuddling over in a corner. I wasn't sure what was going on, so I cleared my throat.

"Hello, are we having a cuddle party?" They both laughed.

"No, silly girl. Cosmo asked me to marry him and I was showing Dax the ring!" Dana said. My heart was in my throat. I thought I was walking in on Dana and Dax betraying Cosmo and I. If that were the case, I'd definitely fall apart and die.

"Oh...." I looked at her ring and smiled, "congratulations. I guess that makes you my sister, huh?" I was happy for them. Ultimately happy. The happiest a girl could be for her twin brother.

"Carina, I have a question I'd like to ask you as well. But, I want to make sure you're okay. You've been out of it all night." Shit. He's done. He's going to leave me.

"Of course I'm okay. I've just been thinking about our time together. It's been such a fantastic time."

"Will you marry me?" Dax didn't spare any words. Straight to the point.

"Uh..." I couldn't speak.

"You waltzed into my life in the ER, strutting your stuff as if you're stupid, but you're the smartest nurse I've ever met. You're caring kind, and everything I've ever wanted. Not to mention you're the only female to ever get me to take time off to go on a date."

"Of course, I will marry you, Dax!" I smiled but my happiness was temporary. This was all temporary.

We celebrated with champagne and watched a movie. Before

long, we went to bed in our room. Cuddling up to him was the highlight of my night. I glanced at the rock on my finger and smiled knowing I found my happiness. I found my purpose. I found my meaning. And I was on the right road to finding myself.

***

COSMO

"What are you doing here, Father?" I asked as I stared into my father's eyes. He wasn't supposed to be here. He's the last person I expected to show up like this. He's the last person I needed to see. We did everything he said but found so much more.

"It's time to return home and take your throne. It's time for the Gemini Twins to rule." Father roared. "Let's go. No time to waste."

"Father, I do not want to go back home. Neither does Carina. We have found our purpose on Earth and our happiness is within the two doors back there. We aren't ready to go back. We still have to finish our assignment." I was hoping this would work. Father wasn't going to give up his throne, unless it was threatened.

Was he sick? Was he affected by the sickness?

"Cosmo, this isn't a request. You need to take the throne. Your sister will be by yourside. The humans will join you in less than a century. You will be able to join them again at another time." Father rambled on. He didn't understand.

We were sent to earth to save the planet, find ourselves and

Finding Happiness

restore the elder god's faith in us, yet Father was telling us to come home now? Something wasn't adding up. The math wasn't mathing.

"What's really going on, father?" I asked him.

"I'm sick. I have caught the sickness and I do not feel like I have much time left. We need to have you and Carina take your oaths and then once you are on the throne, you can return to Earth for the humans." He sighed and explained, "I have about a decade or two left. However, time is different on Earth than it is in Summerlands. So in thirty years, you will need to return and rule your people. Do you understand?" Father was stern, and firm, but always fair.

"What about Mother? Is she not fit to take over the throne during our absence?"

"Your mother faded into the void. I do not feel she will be returning anytime soon." Father sobbed. His eyes were watering, he looked at his hands and desperation filled his aura.

"Okay. I'll do it, but Carina stays with her newfound love. I've never seen her this happy. I will accept the oath on both of our behalf and will return for her in thirty years."

I wasn't sure what I was giving up, but I'd never seen her this happy. She was full of life and joy. She danced while doing dishes. She enjoyed being alive again. Jasper took her happiness away from her teh first time. I wasn't letting anyone else take this light from her again. Including our father.

"Really, you would do that for her son?" Father questioned. He had a strange smile on his face.

"Yes. I would give up my happiness so my sister could be happy and rule our world while she enjoys our happiness. I do know the cost, but this is a sacrifice worth taking. After all, I did all of this for her in the beginning…" I knew what I was giving up. Was I ready to say goodbye to Dana? My happiness was merely temporary anyway. As long as Carina was far, far away from Jasper and smiling, I was happy.

"You passed the test. I will allow the two of you to reign on earth. It makes me happy that this test was successful. Ultimately, that is what all of this was about." Father laughed.

"What test?" Carina and I said at the same time. I wasn't aware she was listening.

"The Pearly Gates were restored. You were able to return home if you didn't have a purpose or find your happiness. Jasper was sent to the Underworld for breaking your heart and taking your chastity before time was deemed appropriate. Also, since he turned several of the demi-goddesses into harlots, we sent the harlots to Earth as well and removed their immortality. They will serve as earthlings too. Their moral compass is what kept our world from thriving. With them gone, you having happiness and purpose, I will rule until you are ready. Also, your mother just woke up. I feel her tugging on our heartstrings."

"Thank you, father." We both said at the same time.

We prepared Dana and Daxter breakfast. Who knew this was going to be the beginning of a love and life they wouldn't have originally had if we hadn't waltzed into their world? Not that they wouldn't have had it if we didn't disrupt their fate, but they were now our destiny, our purpose, our happiness. I wasn't letting anything come in the way of Carina's smile and my happiness.

This world was now ours. Earth would be our new home. I just hope it liked us as much as we liked it. Of course it would, we're the Gemini Twins.

"Good morning, you two! Why are you up so early?" Dana

walked out wrapping her house coat around her waist. She was more and more beautiful every day.

"We're just saving the world one douche at a time," Carina mumbled under her breath.

"I love saving the world!" Daxton chipped in. He wrapped his arms around her waist and she leaned her head back onto his shoulder.

"If saving the world means waking up every day to see you, I'm always on board," Carina said as she kissed his neck.

"We do too, especially if we do it with the both of you." I looked at Carina as she said the most beautiful words.

"Awe, we will do anything for the two of you!"

The lovey-dovey cringe conversation went on for about an hour. We ate breakfast, planned our meals for the next week, and then went to work.

Before long, Carina and Dana found out they were pregnant. They both carried two sets of twins at two different times. We had eight children between us and it was absolutely the greatest life we could have imagined.

"Who knew we could reign on earth after destroying the pearly gates?" Carina looked at me and laughed.

"Who knew we would both walk away from ruling Summerlands and find our ultimate happiness?" I laughed.

"I think the universe knew what it was doing. Find a way to make us save the world. Let us reign on earth, and Summerlands still thrive…. It was the perfect plan…"

To be continued….

Forbidden Love: The Tale of Sarandiel and Adrian

By: Ireland Lorelei
Chapter One: The Meeting
Sarandiel

As an angel, it was my duty to watch over the humans and ensure their safety. I had been flying over a small village when I saw him sitting under a tree, reading a book. His face was illuminated by the sun, and there was a sense of peace and serenity around him. I felt drawn to him, and I flew down to get a closer look.

"Hello," I said, hovering above him. "What are you reading?"

He looked up at me, surprised. "Oh, hello. It's a book about the stars and the constellations. I find it fascinating."

I smiled at him. "I love the stars too. They remind me of home."

"Home?" he repeated, curiously.

Forbidden Love: The Tale of Sarandiel and Adrian

I hesitated, wondering if I should reveal my true identity as an angel. But something about him made me feel comfortable, and I decided to take a chance.

"I'm not from around here," I said. "I'm an angel."

His eyes widened in amazement. "An angel? I've never met one before."

We talked for hours about our interests and beliefs. I was drawn to his kindness, intelligence, and his love for life. I felt a sense of longing that I had never felt before, but I knew it was wrong for an angel to fall in love with a human.

As the sun began to set, I realized I had spent the entire day with him. I had never spent so much time with a human before, and I knew that my fellow angels would not approve.

"I have to go," I said, reluctantly. "It's getting late, and I need to return to heaven."

He looked disappointed. "Will I see you again?"

I hesitated, unsure of how to answer. "I don't know," I said finally. "But I hope so."

As I flew back to heaven, I couldn't stop thinking about him. My heart was filled with a sense of longing that I had never felt before. I knew it was wrong for an angel to fall in love with a human, but I couldn't help the way I felt.

Over the next few weeks, I found myself drawn to him more and more. I would watch him from afar, never daring to reveal my true identity. But I knew I had to be careful. The other angels were suspicious of my behavior, and I couldn't risk being caught.

One day, as I was watching him, he looked up at the sky and smiled.

"I wish I could see the stars up close," he said wistfully.

I knew I had to do something. I flew down to him and said,

"I can show you the stars."

His eyes lit up. "Really? How?"

"Close your eyes," I said. "And hold on to me."

He did as I asked, and together, we flew up into the sky, higher and higher, until we were surrounded by the stars.

His eyes were wide with wonder. "This is incredible," he said.

I smiled at him, feeling a sense of joy that I had never experienced before. It was as if, for a moment, all of the rules and obligations that came with being an angel had faded away.

As we descended back to earth, I knew that I was playing with fire. My feelings for him were growing stronger every day, and I knew that I was risking everything by spending time with him, a human. But my heart had already made its choice, and I couldn't help but wonder what the future held for me and the man I had come to love.

Chapter Two: The Growing Attraction
Adrian

I couldn't stop thinking about the angel I had met. She was the most beautiful creature I had ever seen, and her presence had left me feeling both exhilarated and nervous. I had never felt this way about anyone before, and I found myself wondering about her constantly.

As the days passed, I couldn't shake the memory of the angel from my mind. I went about my daily routine, but my thoughts kept drifting back to her. I longed to see her again, to talk to her, to learn more about her.

Finally, I decided to take a chance. I returned to the spot where I had met the angel, hoping that she would appear again.

To my surprise, she did. She appeared before me, her wings outstretched, her face glowing with an otherworldly light.

"Adrian," she said, smiling at me. "I'm glad to see you again."

I was taken aback. "You remember me?"

She nodded. "Of course I do. How could I forget?"

We talked for hours, discussing everything from the stars to the nature of existence itself. I found myself opening up to her in ways I had never had before. I felt a deep connection to her, as if we were kindred spirits.

As the day began to draw to a close, I realized I didn't want to leave. I was enjoying myself too much, and I didn't want our time together to end.

"I wish we could stay like this forever," I said, looking up at the angel.

She smiled sadly. "I know. But we can't. You have your life, and I have mine."

I felt a pang of sadness in my heart. I knew she was right, but I couldn't help feeling like I wanted more.

Days turned into weeks, and weeks turned into months. I went about my life, but I couldn't shake the memory of the angel from my mind. I found myself constantly looking up at the sky, wondering if she was watching me.

Finally, one day, I saw her again. She appeared before me, her face filled with a sense of urgency.

"Adrian," she said, her voice shaking. "I need to tell you something."

I felt a sense of dread in my heart. I knew that something was wrong.

"What is it?" I asked.

She hesitated. "I…I shouldn't be here. I'm not supposed to be with you. It's against the rules of the gods."

I was confused. "What do you mean?"

"I mean that angels are not supposed to fall in love with

humans," she said, her voice low. "It's forbidden. If we're caught, I could be banished from heaven forever."

I felt a sense of shock wash over me. I had never considered that our friendship was forbidden. I had always assumed that it was just two beings enjoying each other's company.

"I had no idea," I said finally.

She nodded. "I know. But we have to be careful. The other angels are suspicious of me, and if they find out about us…"

She trailed off, but I knew what she meant. We were both in danger.

For the first time, I realized just how deep my feelings for the angel ran. I knew I couldn't bear the thought of losing her.

"We have to do something," I said, determination in my voice. "We can't let them keep us apart."

She looked at me, a mix of fear and sadness in her eyes. "I don't know if there's anything we can do. The rules are clear, and if we break them…"

I interrupted her.

"We'll find a way," I said, my heart pounding with determination. "We can't give up on each other."

The angel looked at me, a hint of a smile on her face. "You're very brave, Adrian. But we have to be careful. If we're caught, the consequences could be dire."

I nodded, understanding the gravity of the situation. "I know. But I can't just sit back and watch as we're torn apart. We have to at least try."

The angel looked at me, her eyes shining with admiration. "You're right. We can't give up on each other. I'll do everything I can to make this work."

I felt a surge of hope in my heart. We were in this together, and we would find a way to be together, no matter what.

Forbidden Love: The Tale of Sarandiel and Adrian

As the sun began to set, the angel said her goodbyes and flew back to heaven. I watched her go, feeling a sense of longing that I couldn't shake.

But I knew that I had to be patient. We had a long road ahead of us, and it wouldn't be easy. But as long as we had each other, we could face anything.

I looked up at the sky, wondering when I would see her again. But no matter how long it took, I knew I would wait for her. Because she was the one I had been waiting for my whole life, and I wasn't about to let her go.

Chapter Three: The Forbidden Kiss
Sarandiel

As I flew back to heaven, I couldn't stop thinking about Adrian. My heart was torn between my duty as an angel and my growing feelings for him. I knew it was forbidden for angels to fall in love with humans, but I couldn't help the way I felt.

Days turned into weeks, and I found myself watching Adrian from afar, never daring to reveal my true identity. But as time passed, my feelings for him grew stronger, and I knew that I had to be careful.

One day, I decided to visit him again. I appeared before him, my wings outstretched, my face glowing with an otherworldly light.

"Hello, Adrian," I said, smiling at him.

He looked up at me, surprised. "Sarandiel! It's good to see you."

We talked for hours, discussing everything from books to the meaning of life. I felt a deep connection to him, and I knew that my feelings for him were only growing stronger.

As the day began to draw to a close, I knew that I had to be careful. I couldn't stay with him for too long, or risk being

Reigning on Earth

discovered.

"I have to go," I said, reluctantly. "But I'll be back soon."

He looked disappointed. "Will I see you again?"

I hesitated, unsure of what to say. "I don't know," I said finally. "But I hope so."

As I flew back to heaven, I couldn't stop thinking about him. I knew that what we were doing was dangerous, but I couldn't help the way I felt. I knew I had to be careful, but I couldn't bear the thought of losing him.

Days turned into weeks, and weeks turned into months. I found myself constantly thinking about Adrian, wondering what he was doing, and longing to be with him.

Finally, one day, I saw him again. He looked up at the sky, and I knew that he was thinking about me.

"Hello, Adrian," I said, appearing before him.

He smiled at me, and my heart skipped a beat. "Sarandiel. It's good to see you again."

We talked for hours, losing track of time as we discussed everything from the stars to the meaning of life. I felt a deep connection with him, and I knew that he felt the same way.

As the sun began to set, I knew that I had to leave. But before I could go, Adrian took my hand.

"Sarandiel, I know that what we're doing is dangerous," he said, his voice trembling. "But I can't help the way I feel about you. I want to be with you, no matter what."

I felt a surge of emotion in my heart. I knew that what he was saying was dangerous, but I couldn't help feeling the same way.

"Adrian, I feel the same way," I said, my voice barely above a whisper. "But we can't be together. It's forbidden."

He looked at me, his eyes pleading. "I know. But I can't

Forbidden Love: The Tale of Sarandiel and Adrian

imagine my life without you. Please, Sarandiel. We have to find a way."

I felt torn between my duty as an angel and my growing feelings for Adrian. I knew that what we were doing was dangerous, but I couldn't help the way I felt.

"Adrian, I want to be with you too," I said finally. "But we have to be careful. We can't let anyone find out about us. The consequences could be dire."

He nodded, understanding the gravity of the situation. "I know. But I can't just let you go. I'll do whatever it takes to be with you."

I looked at him, feeling a mix of fear and excitement. I knew that we were playing with fire, but I couldn't help feeling like we were meant to be together.

"We'll find a way," I said, determination in my voice. "I can't bear the thought of losing you, either. We'll do whatever it takes to be together."

As I flew back to heaven, I knew that our connection was growing stronger every day. But I also knew that we were taking a risk. If we were caught, the consequences could be dire.

Over the next few weeks, I found myself constantly thinking about Adrian. I longed to be with him, to hold him, to kiss him. But I knew that we had to be careful. We couldn't let anyone find out about us.

Finally, one day, I saw him again. He looked up at the sky, and I appeared before him.

"Sarandiel," he said, his eyes filled with longing. "I can't stop thinking about you."

I felt my heart skip a beat. "I feel the same way," I said, my voice barely above a whisper.

He took my hand, and we looked into each other's eyes

"I don't care about the rules," he said, his voice filled with conviction. "I want to be with you. I'll do whatever it takes."

I felt a surge of emotion in my heart. I knew that what he was saying was dangerous, but I couldn't help feeling the same way.

"Adrian, I want to be with you too," I said. "But we have to be careful. We can't let anyone find out about us. The consequences could be dire."

He nodded, his eyes filled with determination. "I know. But we have to try. We can't just sit back and let the rules keep us apart."

I knew that he was right. We couldn't just sit back and do nothing. We had to at least try to be together.

"We'll find a way," I said, my heart pounding with determination. "We can't give up on each other."

It was in that moment that I knew I wanted to be with Adrian in every way possible. I kissed him and he took my mouth, parting my lips and slipping in his tongue. I couldn't keep my hands off of him. I wanted to touch him everywhere and I wanted him to touch every inch of my body. We laid down right where we were and he pressed his lips to my breasts and then trailed them down my stomach.

He looked at me with concern in his eyes and asked, "Are you sure?"

I grabbed the sides of his face with my hands and pulled him to me, "Yes, I am sure."

When he took me and made me his, I had never felt so much love and passion.

After we had both gotten saturated with sweat and I had the most powerful orgasm in all of my years, we laid there, we looked into each other's eyes. It was in that moment that I knew that we were in this together. We would find a way to be together, no matter what.

Chapter Four: The Warning
Adrian

As I sat by Sarandiel's side, watching the sun rise over the horizon, I felt a sense of peace and contentment wash over me. We had built a life together that was full of love and joy, and I knew we were meant to be together.

But as we sat there, basking in the sun's warmth, I sensed that something was wrong. Sarandiel's usually bright and cheerful demeanor had been replaced with a sense of worry and apprehension.

"What's wrong?" I asked, placing my hand on hers.

She sighed, looking out at the vast expanse of the universe. "My fellow angels came to me last night," she said. "They warned me about the consequences of my actions, about the rules of the gods, and how they forbid angels from being romantically involved with humans."

I felt a pang of fear and worry wash over me. I had always known that our love was unique, that it defied the traditional rules and boundaries set by the gods. But to hear that Sarandiel's actions could have serious consequences…it filled me with dread.

"What did they say?" I asked, trying to keep my voice steady.

"They warned me that if I continue to pursue this path, I could face punishment," she said. "They said that I was putting myself and our family in danger, that the gods would not look kindly upon our relationship."

I felt a knot form in my stomach. The thought of Sarandiel

being punished, of our family being torn apart…it was too much to bear.

"What are we going to do?" I asked, my voice filled with worry.

Sarandiel looked at me, her eyes filled with determination. "We're going to continue on our path," she said. "We're going to show the gods and the universe that love knows no boundaries, that it transcends all."

I felt a sense of admiration wash over me. Sarandiel was brave, and she was committed to our love, even in the face of danger and opposition.

And so we continued on our path, working tirelessly to spread our message of love and compassion. We faced opposition from some, and there were those who didn't understand our vision.

But we persisted, knowing that our love was stronger than any obstacle we could encounter.

As time went on, I began to see a change in the world around us. People were starting to come together, to see the value in our message of love and compassion, and to work towards a brighter future.

And even as the warnings of the gods lingered in the back of my mind, I knew that our love would continue to guide us forward.

Together, we had built a life that was full of beauty and possibility, and we would continue to work towards a world that was built on the principles of love, compassion, and empathy.

And as the sun set on our world, I knew that our love would continue to shine, a beacon of hope and possibility that would guide us forward into a bright and beautiful future.

As the days passed, I couldn't help but feel a sense of

unease about the warning we had received. The idea of losing Sarandiel, or worse, facing punishment myself, was too much to bear.

I tried to focus on our work, on spreading our message of love and compassion, but the warning lingered in the back of my mind, a constant reminder of the risks we were taking.

And then, one day, my worst fears were realized. A group of angels appeared before us, their faces stern and unforgiving.

"You have been warned, Sarandiel," one of them said. "Your actions have put yourself and our community in danger. If you continue down this path, there will be consequences."

I felt a sense of dread wash over me as the reality of the situation set in. The risks we had taken, the love we had shared…it had all come to this.

But even in the face of danger, Sarandiel remained steadfast. She refused to be cowed by the angels' warnings, and instead, she stood up for our love, for the vision we had created together.

And slowly but surely, the angels began to see the value in what we were doing. They saw the impact we were having, the change we were creating, and they began to understand that love knew no boundaries.

In the end, our love prevailed. We had faced the greatest of challenges, and we had come out stronger on the other side.

As the sun set on our world, I felt a sense of gratitude wash over me. We had been given a second chance, a chance to continue on our path, to create a world that was full of beauty, hope, and possibility.

And as I looked into the future, I knew that our love would continue to guide us forward, helping us to overcome any obstacle that came our way. We had built a life that was full of joy and purpose, and nothing, not even the warnings of the gods, could stand in our way.

Chapter Five: The Temptation
Sarandiel's

As I gazed out at the vast expanse of the universe, I felt a sense of unease wash over me. Despite our many accomplishments, there was a constant temptation lurking in the back of my mind.

Adrian.

He was the source of my greatest joy and my greatest fear. Our love was a forbidden one, a bond that defied the rules set forth by the gods.

And yet, despite the risks, I couldn't help but be drawn to him. His smile, his touch, his very presence…they filled me with a sense of warmth and contentment that I had never known before.

But the more time we spent together, the greater the risks became. As an angel, I had a position of great responsibility, and my actions could have serious consequences for both myself and those around me.

And yet, despite my better judgment, I found myself constantly drawn to Adrian. His kindness, his intelligence, and his unwavering support of our mission…they were too much for me to resist.

I knew that I was playing with fire, that my actions could have serious consequences. But I couldn't help but feel that our love was worth the risk.

And so, we continued to be together, even as the warnings of my fellow angels lingered in the back of my mind. They cautioned me about the dangers of our love, about the risks it posed to my position as an angel.

But the more they warned me, the more I found myself

Forbidden Love: The Tale of Sarandiel and Adrian

drawn to Adrian. His love filled me with a sense of passion and purpose that I had never known before.

And yet, despite my love for him, I couldn't help but feel a sense of guilt and unease. My actions could have serious consequences, not just for myself, but for those around me.

As I looked out at the universe, I knew that I had a decision to make. I could continue down the path I was on, risking everything for the love I felt for Adrian. Or I could step back, heed the warnings of my fellow angels, and try to find a way to be with him that didn't put my position as an angel in jeopardy.

But no matter how hard I tried, I couldn't shake the feeling that our love was worth any risk, any consequence.

And so we continued to be together, navigating the obstacles and challenges that came our way. Some days were harder than others, and there were times when I felt the weight of the world on my shoulders.

But through it all, Adrian's love remained constant, filling me with a sense of hope and possibility that kept me going.

As I looked into the future, I knew that our love would continue to guide us forward, helping us to navigate the challenges and obstacles that lay ahead.

And even though I knew that my position as an angel was at risk, I couldn't help but feel that our love was worth any sacrifice.

As I continued to grapple with the temptation of being with Adrian, I couldn't help but feel conflicted. On one hand, our love brought me a sense of joy and fulfillment that I had never known before. But on the other hand, I knew that my position as an angel was at risk.

I tried to push the warnings of my fellow angels aside to focus on the love that Adrian and I shared. But as the days went by, I struggled more and more to keep my feelings in check.

The more time we spent together, the stronger my love for him grew. And even as I tried to resist the temptation, I found myself drawn to him, unable to imagine a life without him by my side.

But the more I thought about the risks, the more I realized I couldn't continue down this path. I had a responsibility to the community I served, to my fellow angels, and to the gods.

And so, I made the tough decision to step back, to try to find a way to be with Adrian that didn't put my position as an angel in jeopardy.

It wasn't easy, and there were times when I felt as though I was betraying the love we shared. But I knew that it was the right thing to do, for myself and for our community.

And so we continued to work together, to spread our message of love and compassion. Adrian understood the risks, and he supported my decision, even though it meant that we couldn't be together in the way we wanted.

As the days turned into weeks, I felt a sense of peace wash over me. I knew that our love was still there, still strong and vibrant, even if we couldn't express it in the way we wanted.

And slowly but surely, I began to see a new path forward. A way to be with Adrian that didn't put my position as an angel in jeopardy, a way to continue our love without risking everything we had worked for.

It wasn't perfect, and there were still risks involved. But I knew that our love was worth it, that it was worth taking a chance on.

And so, we continued to work towards a future that was built on the principles of love, compassion, and empathy. We faced challenges and obstacles along the way, but we knew that our love was stronger than any opposition we could encounter.

As the sun set on our world, I knew that our love would continue to guide us forward, helping us to overcome any obstacle that came our way. We had built a life that was full of purpose and meaning, and even though our love was unique, we knew that it was worth any risk or sacrifice.

Chapter Six: The Reprimand
Adrian

As Sarandiel and I continued to work towards a future built on love and compassion, I couldn't help but feel a sense of unease. We had faced warnings from our fellow angels, but now, it seemed, the gods themselves were taking notice of our actions.

I tried to push the thought aside, to focus on the work we were doing, but the sense of dread lingered in the back of my mind.

And then, one day, the gods appeared before us, their faces stern and unforgiving.

"Sarandiel," one of them said, "you have been warned about the consequences of your actions. And yet, you have continued to disobey our laws and put yourself and those around you at risk."

I felt a sense of fear wash over me as the gods spoke, their voices booming and powerful. I knew that we had taken risks, that our love had put us in a precarious position, but I had never imagined that the gods themselves would take notice.

But Sarandiel remained steadfast, refusing to be cowed by

the reprimand. She stood up to the gods, defending our love and the work we had done.

And slowly but surely, the gods began to see the value in what we were doing. They saw the impact we were having, the change we were creating, and they began to understand that love knew no boundaries.

But even as they began to soften, I couldn't help but feel a sense of fear and unease. The gods had immense power, and if they decided to punish us for our disobedience, there was little we could do to stop them.

And yet, despite my fear, I knew that our love was worth any risk. I knew that the work we were doing was important, that it was changing the world for the better.

And so, we continued on, even as the threat of punishment hung over our heads. We worked harder than ever before, spreading our message of love and compassion to every corner of the universe.

As the days turned into weeks, I began to feel a sense of hope wash over me. The gods had not punished us, and it seemed as though they were beginning to understand the importance of our work.

But even as our love continued to guide us forward, I couldn't shake the feeling that the threat of punishment still loomed over us.

And so, we continued to work towards a future built on love and compassion, even as we faced the constant threat of retribution from the gods.

As the sun set on our world, I knew that our love would continue to guide us forward, helping us to overcome any obstacle that came our way. We had built a life that was full of purpose and meaning, and even though our love was unique,

Forbidden Love: The Tale of Sarandiel and Adrian

we knew that it was worth any risk or sacrifice.

The warning from the gods continued to weigh heavily on my mind, even as we continued our work towards a better future. I couldn't shake the feeling that we were constantly being watched, that any misstep could result in punishment.

And yet, despite the risks, I knew that our love was worth it. It had brought me a sense of happiness and fulfillment that I had never known before, and I couldn't imagine a life without Sarandiel by my side.

But as the days turned into weeks, I began to notice a shift in our relationship. Sarandiel seemed more distant, more preoccupied with the risks we were taking.

I tried to ignore the changes, to focus on the love we shared, but the unease continued to grow.

And then, one day, Sarandiel approached me with a look of sadness in her eyes.

"I need to leave," she said. "The risks are too great, and I can't continue to put myself and those around me in danger."

I felt a sense of despair wash over me as she spoke, realizing that our love was once again being threatened by the forces that were beyond our control.

But even as I tried to protest, to convince her to stay, I knew deep down that she was making the right decision. The risks were too great, and I couldn't bear the thought of her being punished for our love.

And so, Sarandiel left, disappearing into the sky with a heavy heart and a sense of sadness that weighed heavily on my own heart.

As the days turned into weeks, I struggled to come to terms with her absence. The love we had shared was still there, still strong and vibrant, but it seemed as though the risks had finally caught up with us.

And then, one day, she returned. Her face was filled with a sense of joy and relief, and I knew in that moment that something had changed.

"The gods have blessed us," she said. "They have seen the value in our work, and they have given us their blessing to continue down this path."

I felt a sense of hope wash over me as she spoke, realizing that our love was once again free to thrive, to guide us towards a future that was built on compassion and empathy.

And so, we continued on, working harder than ever before to spread our message of love and understanding. We faced challenges and obstacles along the way, but we knew that our love was worth any risk or sacrifice.

As the sun set on our world, I knew that our love would continue to guide us forward, helping us to overcome any obstacle that came our way. We had built a life that was full of purpose and meaning, and even though our love was unique, we knew that it was worth any risk or sacrifice.

To Be Continued

Author Bio

She is from a small coastal town in North Carolina and currently resides in Florida. She started reading romance novels, watching soap operas and romance/drama movies with her mother as a teenager. She then started enjoying horror, mystery, and thrillers. Her imagination and creativity started her to write her own romance novels.

Forbidden Love: The Tale of Sarandiel and Adrian

Ireland started writing contemporary romance and contemporary with a little erotica and spread her wings into dark romance, reverse harem and paranormal romance.

She has written the following Series:
   Seals and Bounty (7 Books) - Dark Romance
   Second Chance (5 Books) - Contemporary with Erotica
   Vegas Blue written in Susan Stokers World (4 Books) - Contemporary
   The Powerful & Kinky Society (On Going) – Dark Billionaire Romance

She has written the following Standalone's:
   Anonymous Love - Contemporary
   Don't Tap Out (Part 1) & Don't Tap Out Again (Part 2) - Dark Romance
   Entangled (Part 1) & UnEntangled (Part 2) - Contemporary with Erotica
   From the Ashes - Dark Romance
   Island Christmas - Contemporary
   Just Breathe - Dark Romance
   Naughty or Nice - Cuffs, Clamps & Candle Wax - Dark Romance
   Secret Spark - Dark Romance
   Raven – Dark Paranormal Romance

She has written in Anthologies:
   Friends to Lovers
   Mistletoe Kisses
   Lovely Benefits

She published a collection of her short stories in "Dreams Come True" and she released her first "Authors Planner" in 2022.
www.irelandlorelei.com

The Fall of Fire

By: W.A. Ashes
Dedication
Dedicated to Zayne, who's never let his disability stop him from pursuing his passions. You're going to go far, kid.

Trigger Warning
This story is based on the Greek stories of Hephaestus, Ares, Aphrodite, Zeus, Hera, and Eros. Like the ancient tales, there are mentions of infidelity and abuse in this story. If you are believer in the Greek gods, I do not mean to offend you or your deities. Characters from the old stories are used in a factious manner.

Chapter One

Reigning on Earth

The day he fell was the day he found redemption for a sin he never committed. It was the day he found freedom. It was storming that day, like it always did when his father was angry. Mount Olympus was surrounded by a vortex of flickering, grey clouds. Within the gold and marble walls of the palace, his father, the king of the gods, sat upon a cumulus throne. His eyes flashed like lightning, his features were drawn down, sagging with discontentment. Long white hair blew around him as a strong wind swept through the palace. Had those gathered not been gods themselves, the wind would have thrown them off their feet.

Hera's throne of peacock feathers and matching gems sat unoccupied next to Zeus, who was listening to his sons argue about an impending war. Ares had requested the audience with their father, after one of his soldiers reported tremors in the mortal realm. He was convinced one of their ancient ancestors were waking from the slumber the original gods put them in. Titans, after all, could not be destroyed, only contained.

Hephaestus didn't argue with his brother's logic, but he did protest when Ares demanded he re-equip and armor his celestial army. The god of blacksmiths had all of Olympus to arm, after all, and there was a small pile of dysfunctional equipment waiting for him to restore at his forge. He didn't have time to play manservant for Ares. Zeus, however, was much like Hera and had never favored Hephaestus.

"You are absolutely sure it's Pallus?" Zeus confirmed for the third time during the meeting.

"Yes, Father," Ares growled, his eyes flashing red. Ares, who rivaled their father in height and looked like a younger version of the king of gods, met Zeus's hard gaze with his own unyielding one. Hephaestus would never tell his brother, for it

The Fall of Fire

would surely earn him a beating, but Ares was a mini version of the god who sired them. His hair may have still been black, his eyes may have not been guarded by crow's feet, and he may have favored leather jackets over suits, but his disposition was pure Zeus. It always had been. Even when they were children, Ares took what he wanted, when he wanted it, while Hephaestus was left standing in his shadow, forced to be content with his brother's scraps. The one times Hephaestus had convinced their father to favor him, his brother still won in the end and now his wife kept Ares' bed warm instead of their own.

"My soldiers and I are prepared to go to war," Ares continued, locking his hands behind his back like a good little solider, despite the defiance in the raising of his chin.

Hephaestus fought back an eye roll. When wasn't Ares ready to go to war? His brother was born with a thirst for battle.

"I only await your blessing," Ares stated.

Zeus stroked his beard. "If it is Pallus, we cannot risk an uprising. Once one titan awakens, it is easier for the next to do so. I will check with Hades to ensure he has not seen any movement from the ones contained in his realm. As for your war, you have my blessing. Hephaestus, give Ares all the armor and weapons he asks for."

Ares smirked at his brother tauntingly. "I want completely new gear. I won't go against a titan with old materials."

Hephaestus's eyes bulged. He stuttered, "C-completely new? I have a line of other Olympians waiting for their own equipment orders. If I have to recraft armor and weapons for your entire army, I'll never get to leave the forge. Aphrodite is returning home today from a visit to the mortal realm with Eros. I haven't seen her in months and was planning a special dinner for our anniversary. It's rare she is home, father, and I wish to keep her company, so she does not become bored with our dwelling. I can repair what's broken and be sure each item is up to standard for Ares's troops."

"No," It was Zeus's booming voice that shook the throne room. "You will forge new equipment."

"I..."

"Your place is in the forges and your duty is to supply Olympus," Zeus interrupted. "Your work must come before your desire to bed your wife."

Hephaestus wanted to point out that Zeus wasn't exactly the family man the human media made him out to be and he'd often times put his carnal desires over his duty, but he kept his mouth shut in favor of sparing his body an electric shock.

"I can keep Dite company," Ares grinned. Hephaestus wanted to punch him. "So, she doesn't get bored."

Zeus nodded his approval. "It's settled. Ares will entertain Aphrodite while you, Hephaestus, tend to your forge. She can visit you at work if she chooses too, but I want to see at least an eighth of Ares's army outfitted in new gear by the end of the week."

The end of the week was an absurd deadline, even with Hephaestus's cyclops employees he'd won from Poseidon in a poker game. However, Hephaestus could not openly refute his king and father. Zeus would make a public example of him if he were to do so.

Aphrodite hated the forges. She complained the soot ruined her dresses and dried out her skin. She'd never visit, and Ares would end up making love to his brother's wife in their bed.

Dejected, Hephaestus returned to his forge. He threw his tools off their bench and toppled an anvil in his anger. The steady clanging of the cyclops at work stilled as their boss slid

The Fall of Fire

down the wall and crumbled into a shaking ball.

"Get back to work," he managed to choak out after allowing himself a few moments to collect himself. The problem with the forge is that even with the cyclops he was alone. No one talked to him and as he pushed aside Eros's bow, waiting to be restrung, and pulled out a bar of Olympian gold to start work on Ares's order, his mind began to wander.

What if for once he didn't do what he was told? What if instead of letting his father and Ares walk over him he forged a new path outside of the fires he worked with? What if he fell?

He was tired of being used and unloved. His wife openly cheated on him with his brother, his father wanted him locked away beneath Olympus, his stepson only ever came to see him when his equipment needed to be fixed, and his own mother had tried to kill him at birth. What if he changed the story? What if he put himself in the narrative?

Hephaestus had enough. He could work himself to death and no one would care…except Hades, who would put him to work in the Underworld's forges the moment he entered his realm. No. He would no longer be a steppingstone in the myths his family created.

With new resolve, Hephaestus straightened his shoulders and started work on one last project. Using tweezers and his favorite pair of magnifying glasses, for the first time in history he created something for himself. When he was done, he wiped his face with a rag and looked down at the watch with pride.

The watch didn't look like much. It had a simple leather band and gold clockface, but inside rested a special mechanism crafted from crystal gears that would disrupt an Olympian's ability to locate him. The watch would give even Hermes, the god of messages and travelers, a run for his money. Not even the huntress Artemis would be able to find him once he latched the watch around his wrist.

Three days after Zeus gave him the order to help Ares, Hephaestus stood at the edge of Olympus, on the very ledge his mother once threw him off of, but this time he jumped.

Chapter Two

The earth shook when Hephaestus fell. His bones creaked as the dirt pillowed around him, forming a crater a meteorite would be jealous of. For a moment he couldn't move. His body locked up and his metal knee brace hissed from breaks in its hoses. He was used to numbness. He hadn't been able to feel half of his face and below his waist since he was an infant. The tingling sensation in his toes and fingers was new, however, and he found that when he sat up a sharp pain shot through his lower limbs, centering in the middle of his back. A ragged moan escaped his perpetually chapped lips. It'd been centuries since he'd last been out of Olympus and he forgot how painful it was to be in a mortal vessel. How restricting it felt, like his skin was too tight. He wished the dirt and grime from his forge hadn't lingered on his mortal flesh for it irritated him.

Above him, lightning flashed, and thunder rolled. Green leaves whispered about the man who'd fallen from the sky. He held his breath, waiting for a sign that the gods had noticed his disappearance. Nothing happened and he let out a laugh of relief. So long as his watch was intact, no Olympian would be able to find him. He was free.

Hephaestus struggled to move. At first his legs appeared to be useless. He had no intention of using his Olympian powers when he fell, but without their aid he knew he wouldn't make

The Fall of Fire

it out of the crater, let alone to a town to start fresh in.

Reaching out with his power, he willed his clothing, broken brace, and massive bronze hammer to take a form suitable to his current state. His dirty toga changed into a pair of jeans, a Henley, and an unbuttoned plaid shirt. The brace on his knee shrunk into a less chunky, black elastic contraption with metal rods built in to stabilize his leg and his hammer took a simpler form.

Though his limbs still hurt, and dirt still clung to his dark curls and beard, his power settled into his new skin, allowing him to thread the carpenter hammer through a loop on his pants. He already missed the weight of the hammer's previous blacksmith form.

Hephaestus stumbled his way out of the crater. Rain began to fall in fat, hard droplets, leaving streaks on his dirty skin, but he continued to climb. He'd landed in a forested area but could see a highway through the trees once he mounted the lip of the crater. The trail his limp left in the quickly moistening earth made him uneasy. He reminded himself that his watch should mask its presence from the Olympians, but he'd feel better once he got to concrete, where trails would be harder to create.

He grumbled under his breath when a tree limb raked across his face, leaving a deep gash across his cheek. His bad leg caught on an exposed tree root, and he tripped, undoing what little cleansing the rain had given him.

Hephaestus pulled himself up. Mud was smeared across his pants legs, and he scowled at the wetness it left behind. He was no stranger to grime, but he hated the feeling of wet fabric.

The forest gave way to a highway that cut through the forest like a great anaconda. Its surface was marred with tar patches, cracks, and potholes. A sign declared "Now entering Lafayette

County". A state seal was stamped under the words, but Hephaestus was unfamiliar to the location it was associated with. He knew he'd fallen on America, simply because he'd intended to land there. Mount Olympus, after all, existed in a realm between all others. It hovered in the great universe while simultaneously existing and not existing. Those who left Olympus, through either a portal or jumping from one of its ledges, needed to only think of a place in the mortal realm and that's where they would appear.

Hephaestus had chosen America because its culture was too diverse to be considered familiar territory for him. His father and brother, should they or any of the other Olympians, choose to follow him, they wouldn't think to search America first. They'd consider his creature of habit tendencies and look in Greece, which made America the perfect place to hide, for the time being.

The god of the forge limped past the county sign with a slight rush to his steps. The rain had begun to pick up and, judging by the water tower he spotted in the distance, he wasn't too far from a town. If he was lucky, he'd reach civilization before the storm's full power was released.

Though money wasn't something Hephaestus had a lot of, he'd thought ahead and stolen one of the gold cards his brethren used when they came to the mortal realm. Technically there was no monetary value on the thin piece of gold, but he'd crafted it to trick human technology into thinking there was. Fingering the card in his pocket, he briefly wondered how many of the world's economic crisis his kind were responsible for. He would try to be more responsible than the others. He would only use the card when necessary to secure a modest place to stay. Afterall, unlike his wife, who favored the penthouses of New

The Fall of Fire

York, London, and Beijing, all he desired was a table to sit at and a bed to sleep in.

Hephaestus continued his walk along the highway until he crested a hill. His bushy brows drew together when he spotted an old car with faded blue paint parked at the bottom. The car's hazards were on and the blinking orange lights seemed to be beckoning him closer.

Carefully, he made his way down the hill and the closer he got to the car, the more he noticed. The car's plates read, "Missouri". A woman was kneeling on the passenger side, putting her entire weight onto a four-way lug wrench. Her tight curls were drenched, and her clothes were starting to cling to her ebony skin. She was beautiful and frustrated.

Hephaestus's gaze softened as he saw her nose crinkle. She tossed the lug wrench on the ground and kicked the severely flat tire. Another tire, obviously a spar, sat in the grass on the side of the road.

Thunder continued to growl but Hephaestus let the thought of a warm room flee his mind. This woman, whoever she was, was in distress and visibly shaken. He continued walking towards her as she muttered to herself.

"Miss," he said when he was close enough for her to hear him. "Can I help?"

She narrowed her eyes and folded her arms. Giving him a once over, she bit the corner of her lip.

He raised his hands in peace. "I'm on my way to the next town and don't mean any harm."

She sighed and held out a slender hand. There were grease marks on her fingers and calluses on her palm. "I'm Kiara. I'm sorry, I haven't seen you around here before. Are you some kind of hitchhiker?"

Hephaestus frowned. "I..I guess you could say I'm a wanderer. I don't want anything from you, ma'am. I only want to help. My name's...," he hesitated. Could he tell the woman, Kiara, his name without bringing more suspicion to himself? Running a hand through his hair, he settled on saying, "I'm Hep. I'm a mechanic. Let me help?"

Kiara stepped aside, motioning for him to give the tire his best shot. Kneeling by the wheel, he let out a long whistle. Up close, the rubber of the tire was shredded. Parts of it were so bare that he was shocked she hadn't ended up on the side of the road sooner.

Looking over the spare, Hephaestus could tell it was old and had been used before, perhaps even several times. He picked up the lug wrench and stroked his beard.

"I can get you back on the road, but you're going to want to see your mechanic as soon as possible. Your spare's worn and your rim is bent." He circled the car, kicking the back driver side tire. "You're about to lose this one too."

Kiara sighed, slumping against her vehicle. "Great, more money. Look, if you change the tire, I'll give you a ride into town. Lexington is only a few miles and I'm heading there anyway."

"I'd appreciate that, but like I said before, I'm not seeking your aid," he tells her.

"It's the least I can do," she stated, watching as he knelt to begin work on her tire.

The muscles in his arms bulged as he pulled the lug wrench, making the task she'd struggled with look easy. She bit her lip again. She knew nothing about the man helping her. He was clearly without a home and a job if he was wandering along the highway. He seemed nice enough. Yes, she'd repay him by driving him into town and dropping him off at the local motel.

Hephaestus made quick work of the tire and soon enough he was seated in the passenger seat of Kiara's car. They drove in an oddly comforting silence into Lexington, listening to radio weather alerts and rain hit the windshield. When she pulled in front of a sun-faded motel, Hephaestus was almost reluctant to leave her presence.

"Thank you," she said as he made to leave the vehicle.

He offered her a kind smile and she noted the way his tanned, olive skin crinkled around his eyes. There was something warm and steady about his eyes. She had a lot of worries, her car being the least of them, but his gaze calmed her soul.

"Be blessed," he said, holding onto the car door longer than necessary.

For a moment, she watched him go; watching as he walked through the motel doors and wishing she'd offered him a job at her bed and breakfast. She could use a mechanic around her place, but she didn't know him. It would have been stupid to invite a man she'd met on the side of the road into the space she and her son inhabited. As a single mom, she needed to be careful.

Chapter Three

After using his card to obtain a room at the motel, Hephaestus enjoyed a night's sleep. Being a god, he didn't need sleep, food, or even restrooms, but he'd learned over the years to enjoy rest where he could get it. The taste of culinary creations was also something he loved.

In the morning, he stopped by a diner to enjoy a plate of eggs and hash browns. Around him people laughed and chatted with the familiarity that only small towns could provide.

A young man wearing a bandana on his head, poured Hephaestus his coffee and offered him a copy of the local newspaper. The god gave him his thanks and a opened the paper to look at the wanted ads, for he could see himself staying in Lexington for a while. The atmosphere was contagious and so different from what he was used to.

Down the street from his hotel and the diner, was a volunteer ran movie theater, which still used the nostalgic 'r' before the 'e' spelling in its government name. The Rifle Theatre was looking for a part-time janitor. The grocery store was hiring freight workers and a dentist office was looking for a clerk.

At the very bottom of the wanted ads, was a simple listing that was less than a paragraph long.

Wanted – Part-time handy man. Battle Bed and Breakfast. Main Street. Minimal pay. Room and Board offered.

A complete address or phone number weren't given, but the ad sparked Hephaestus's interest. Being a handy man would let him utilize his skills and he didn't need much money, especially if room and board were being offered.

"Hey," he called to the young man who had filled his coffee and was now cleaning the counter.

"What's up?" the boy asked with a dimpled grin.

Hephaestus tapped the listing in the paper. "Battle Bed and Breakfast is hiring a handy man. Do you have their address?"

"Oh, yeah." The young man scribbled an address on a napkin and handed it to his customer. "Mrs. Smith runs the place. She's a nice lady but the building is falling apart. If you're looking for work, you might want to try Arnold's. I've heard Smith is offering basically nothing."

"Room and board ain't nothing."

"It is if you already live in town. If you ask me, she should just sell the place. It ain't worth the work. Building's been around since the Civil War. It isn't a marked historical site, though. Nothing special about it, really. It was just a family home until Mr. Smith renovated it into a bed and breakfast when they moved to town."

Hephaestus went back to eating his breakfast as the young man was called over to a table. An elderly couple were wanting to order one of the specials. For a moment, he merely watched the young man work. There was something surreal about this little town. Maybe it was the fact that he hadn't had a break in…well, since the beginning of time, but he enjoyed the way everyone around him wasn't in a hurry.

Finishing his breakfast and coffee, he folded up the newspaper and slipped it into the back pocket of his jeans. He'd need to stop by a store later to get more clothes, for he knew it wasn't common for humans to wear the same outfit each day of their lives. He, himself, had grown up with the same bronze toga. He wondered what freshly washed clothes would feel like. Would they feel different from his toga when he magicked it clean?

Though he wasn't in a rush, Hephaestus wanted to use his gold card as little as possible. If he wanted to remain hidden on Earth, he needed to make sure not to act like his brethren. This meant he needed a job. So, with the newspaper in his pocket, he paid his bill at the diner, leaving the young man a 50% tip. The bell above the diner door chimed as he left and the elderly couple he'd been watching waved goodbye to him.

Lexington's streets were interesting. Some of them were paved while others were made of brick. The town showed signs of a battle, with the names of businesses hinting at a bloody history. The courthouse had a cannonball lodged in it and Hephaestus felt an overwhelming wave of protection form inside of him. What had his brother done to this quaint little haven? What horrors had his craft unleashed on them? He wanted to scoop the town up and hide it from Ares as if he were a child and it was his favorite teddy bear.

He wandered the town aimlessly for a while, getting to know its layout. Then, when it was close to noon, he headed back to Main Street. Battle Bed and Breakfast was just down the street from the diner. He could stop in to speak to the owner about a job and then pick up something for lunch.

The young man at the diner hadn't been kidding when he said the bed and breakfast needed repair. The two-story, Victorian style home had a porch that looked dangerous to cross with rotting boards and a broken railing. The shutter of an upstairs window had fallen off and was lying in a bush.

Hephaestus made a mental note of the repairs as he carefully walked up the porch steps, which groaned beneath his sturdy weight. The mailbox was faded, the siding needed new paint, and there was a crack in the foundation that definitely needed to be looked at.

A faux wreath welcomed him at the door, which was painted a pleasant purple. He knocked on the door, not knowing the protocol for a bed and breakfast, and waited until the door opened to reveal someone who instantly made him smile.

"Kiara," he greeted.

She blinked at him, then opened the door wider. "Hep? What are you doing here?"

He cleared his throat at the hostility in her tone. "I'm sorry. Did I interrupt something? I'm looking for the owner or manager. I saw an ad in the newspaper and…"

"You're interested in the handyman position?" her eyes grew

wide and her shoulders slumped in what Hephaestus thought looked an awful lot like relief. "I-um, come in. I'm the the owner. Kiara Smith."

She wiped a floured hand on her pants before holding it out for Hephaestus to shake.

"Truly? If I didn't know any better, I'd say the fates are determined to intertwine our destinies." He said it jokingly, but inside he was a little worried that maybe the old bats *were* meddling in his life.

Kiara laughed dryly. "Maybe. I don't believe in fate, but I'll admit I was kicking myself yesterday, thinking I should have offered you the job when you fixed my tire."

"It looks like you have a lot of things that need fixing," he remarked, glancing around the entryway at yellowed wallpaper and old shag carpet.

She ran a hand through her curls and a weight fell upon her shoulders. "Yeah. Too much. Look, Hep, I really need a good handyman to help me fix up this place, but I can't pay much. I'll be honest, business is bad. I'm barely making ends meet by baking cakes for birthday parties. I can't pay more than $800 a month, but I can offer you free room and board to go with it. You won't have to worry about food. You'll be able to eat with my son and I. Of course, that's pending a background check by the state."

Hephaestus frowned. "A background check?"

"Yeah, I got to make sure you don't have any felonies and won't hurt my kid or me," she said.

"I promise I won't, but a background check is impossible," he told her.

She narrowed her eyes and crossed her arms. "Why? Got something to hide?"

Reigning on Earth

"No," he rushed and then stammered, "I-it's just…"

How was he supposed to explain to Kiara that he didn't technically exist? She could run every kind of background check imaginable on him, but she wouldn't get any results.

"Okay," he sighed, giving in to the idea that though this job seemed perfect for him he might not have it for very long. "I'll give you my information, but can I start work while you wait for the check's results? I need the job."

She bit her lip, something he was starting to realize she did a lot. After a few moments, she nodded. "Fine. But only because we haven't had hot water in a week. Can you start today?"

"Yes. Absolutely," he said.

"Wonderful," she said as she glanced at a clock. "Have you eaten lunch?"

"No. I was going to stop by the diner after I spoke with you."

She nodded. "I have a couple of cakes to drop off. If you'd like to ride along, we can get something from the diner for lunch and then I can take you back to the motel for you to finish up any business you have there. As I said, I have a room for you here…so long as you aren't going to murder my family."

He snorted. "Trust me, Kiara, I'm not the violent type. I'm just looking for some peace in my existence."

Chapter Four

Settling into Battle Bed and Breakfast was easy, since Hephaestus didn't have many material possessions. When Kiara showed him his room, he was pleased to find a quilt covering a twin-sized bed, a lamp, a dresser, and a nightstand. It was quaint and the window looked out over the back of the lawn, where he could see the old iron fence and ivy vines that were trying their hardest to overtake it.

Kiara gave him a tool belt and toolbox. She showed him around the house and the garage. It was a brief but effective tour and by the time she left to pick up her son from school, Hephaestus was confident enough to start work. After all, she'd said there hadn't been hot water for a week.

The water heater was located under the home, in an unfinished basement. The floor was concrete and it was stained with spilled paint. Wooden hooks stored brooms, rakes, and other cleaning items on the walls. An old coal shoot was boarded up, but not properly insulated. He added its insulation to his ever-growing mental list of repairs.

The water heater itself was jammed in a corner, making hissing and gurgling sounds that a heater shouldn't make. Honestly, all he had to do was look at the contraption to know it was severely out of date and needed a complete replacement. The financial situation of Battle Bed and Breakfast didn't favor replacing it, however. He hoped he was skilled enough to convince it to keep working without having to use his Olympian abilities.

Kiara had told him that she'd get a debit card for him to purchase anything he needed for repairs, but if she couldn't afford to pay her employee more than $800 a month, she certainly couldn't afford to drop over $1,000 on a new water heater. Thankfully for her, Hephaestus knew a thing or two about refurbishing technology.

With his tool belt resting on his hips and his hammer slipped into one of its loops, Hephaestus set to work on the water heater. It didn't take him long to realize what the problem was. The top heating element was busted. It looked old enough to be an antique, so it wasn't shocking. Though the lower heating element was still working, it most likely didn't have much life left in it either.

Hephaestus dug a small notebook and pencil out of his handy belt and wrote down the parts he'd need to get the water heater up and running. He'd spotted a hometown hardware store. They should either have the parts he needed in stock or be able to order them.

A screen door slammed shut and someone raced across the floor above him, making dust and dirt rain down on the former god's head.

"Zion!" Kiara called out. "What have I told you about leaving your backpack in front of the door!"

Zion. That was an interesting name. Mount Zion was as important to Christian mythology as Mount Olympus was to Greek mythology. He wondered if Kiara was religious or if she picked the name for her child because she liked how it sounded. It was an old word and like all old words, it held a power that humans didn't fully understand.

"Zion! Come here! I need to introduce you to someone… Hep? Hep, you inside?" she yelled.

Hephastus cleaned up his workspace and headed back upstairs, where he found Kiara in the kitchen putting groceries away. A small, dirty sneaker was on the floor by the island and a bookbag was tossed haphazardly over the back of a stool.

"Hey," Kiara greeted, blowing a curl out of her eyes.

"Hey. I looked at the water heater," he told her.

Her eyes bulged. "Already? Have you gotten to settle in?"

He shrugged. "I like work. The heater is an old model, but we should be able to find parts. I have a list." He placed the notepad on the island. She picked up the paper and read over his scratchy words.

The Fall of Fire

When she handed the notepad back, it was with a shy smile. "I'm going, to be honest, I don't know what any of that is. I called the bank and we're getting you a card set up for parts and stuff. My husband had an account at Harvey's Hardware. I'll call down to have it reopened tomorrow. If you get your parts from there, they'll charge the account and I'll pay it at the end of each month. You can use the card for any tools or things you need to order online. Harvey's doesn't carry much. Just the basics. At least that's what Simon used to say."

"Simon?" Hephaestus couldn't help but ask.

"My husband," she replied.

He nodded. "Do I need to run any of my purchases by him?"

"Oh," her face scrunched up, "no. He…he's dead."

Hephaestus literally drew back in shock. "I'm sorry."

"It's okay. It's…it's been a year now," She sighed and bit her lip. "He was a good man. Probably too good, since it was his hero complex that got him killed."

Hephaestus had known many heroes throughout history. He'd forged weapons for Hercules, Perseus, Odysseus, and more. All their stories, no matter who they were, ended the same way. A hero's life wasn't a fairy tale. It always ended in tragedy.

He nodded his understanding. "I'm sorry. I know it's hard to lose someone you love. I'm sure his sacrifice wasn't in vain."

The way Kiara tilted her head was cute. Hephaestus couldn't help the way his heart fluttered. She reminded him of a fox. She was beautiful and strong, and there was something mysterious about her.

"It wasn't. He was a firefighter. He died saving a little girl. You've lost someone too?"

He shifted uncomfortably. "Not to death, but sometimes it

feels like I have. My…wife…she…"

"You don't have to tell me," she said.

"You told me about Simon," he told her.

She shrugged. "It's okay. If it's hard to talk about, I won't force you to. Grief is soul consuming."

"It is. Dite and I weren't supposed to get married. She was in love with my brother, and I was in love with her. I thought my parents were showing me kindness when they arranged our marriage, but it turned into a living hell. She never loved me and she's publicly with my brother."

"I'm so sorry. That's…That's horrible. I can't imagine being in a loveless marriage. Simon and I were college sweethearts. We…"

"Mom!" A young boy zipped around the corner, nearly colliding with Hephaestus. "Oh, I'm…who are you?"

"Hey, kid." Hephaestus couldn't help but smile. It'd been a very long time since he'd seen a child. The last was Eros, Aphrodite, and Ares's son. The boy had liked to watch him the forge when he was younger but, like all gods, he grew quickly and in modern times he paid little mind to anything that was outside his realm of rulership. "I'm Hep."

"That's a weird name," the kid stated. He looked a little like Kiara, but his jaw was sharper, his nose was pointed, and his skin was slightly darker than his mom's. The boy's curls were shaved short, and he wore a simple pair of basketball shorts and a t-shirt.

"It's a nickname. Short for Hephaestus."

The boy giggled. He couldn't be more than eight years old. "That's an even weirder name."

"Be nice," Kiara interrupted with a fond smile. "Hep is here to help us. He'll be living here as our new handyman."

The Fall of Fire

"Oh, okay. I'm Zion!"

"It's nice to meet you, Zion." Hephaestus grinned, shaking the small hand the boy held out to him.

Zion hopped onto one of the stools. "So, you like fixing things? I like fixing things too. I've been trying to fix my bike, but Mom keeps making me stop."

"Because you kept cutting yourself on the chain," Kiara interjected.

Zion ignored her. "When I grow up, I want to be an engineer. So, I have to get good at fixing things."

"An engineer? That's a big word for a little boy."

"I'm not little," the boy challenged. "I'm seven."

"Well, then, young man," Hephaestus's grin grew, "I think engineering is a fine job choice for you. If you want, I can look at your bike. Maybe I can show you how to fix it."

Zion twirled so violently to face his mom that the stool almost toppled over. "Can he Mom? Please?"

Part of Hephaestus lit up at the thought of teaching the boy how to fix his bike. He'd always wanted a son, but Aphrodite refused him, children. Then, when he'd asked for an apprentice, Zeus laughed at him.

"I guess," Kiara answered. "I don't see why that'd be a problem. For now, though, why don't you take your things upstairs and wash up for dinner? I picked up a rotisserie chicken, potatoes, and mac and cheese for dinner."

Zion made a loud, "Yippee!" sound and jumped off the stool to gather his dirty sneakers and backpack. When he was gone, Hephaestus helped Kiara set the table. They worked in a silence that was as oddly comfortable as their car ride into town.

Later that night, as Hephaestus readied for bed, he took a moment to look out his window and up at the night sky. He wondered if beyond those clouds, above the realm of mortals, if his family had noticed his absence yet. Had his wife come home and looked to greet him or had she fallen straight into Ares's embrace? What of his father? His mother? Had they realized the fires deep in the belly of Olympus had gone out? If so, he doubted they cared.

Chapter Five

As far as gods and goddesses went, Eros was a baby. Though he looked to be in his early twenties and had existed for centuries upon centuries, most Olympians still saw him as a child. His parents thought he was irresponsible; they'd even gone as far as to curse him as a form of punishment when he went against their wishes. His grandparents saw his job as 'cute', like he was a toddler following his mom around, playing office. He was the god of love, for Zeus's sake. He deserved more respect. At the very least, he deserved his own place on the mount. Even Artemis who was permanently twelve had her own home, but Eros had to live with his parents. He kept a room at both Ares's and Aphrodite's home, though he secretly favorited the one at his mother's. His stepfather, after all, was the only Olympian who ever seemed to take him seriously.

Falling onto his bed, he sighed as the pillows and comforter cradled him. The home was unusually cool. With it being built directly atop the forges, Hephaestus's work usually kept it hot. Aphrodite would complain, saying the heat was too dry.

It was a rare occurrence for Eros to be home. Lately, he'd been overwhelmed in the mortal realm. War and love went hand in hand, after all, and as his father's followers wreaked the world, he nurtured its hope using his arrows. Speaking of which, he'd

The Fall of Fire

need to stop by the forges in the morning. Hephaestus had his favorite bow and promised he'd have it restrung the next time Eros visited.

When he was little, Eros used to love the forges. Hephaestus had always felt more like a dad than an uncle to him. He was callous and rough, like Ares, but his eyes were softer, and his parenting style was gentle. Where Ares had a live and learn attitude, Hephaestus believed in the art of trade work. He believed that nurturing another person's abilities was one of the greatest things a being could do.

It'd been too long since Eros had asked to help his stepfather in the forges. If the god hadn't already restrung his bow, perhaps he'd ask him to teach him how…again. The truth of the mater was that he didn't need the god of the forge to fix his prized bow. He knew how to maintain his equipment, but playing the air head who couldn't ever remember how granted him a short reprieve in the forges whenever he was home. His time in the forges was one of the few things he looked forward to when returning home.

There was a knock on his bedroom door and Eros rolled his head to the side to look at the contraption. He didn't answer, but he didn't need to because his mother spoke without entering.

"Eros, I'm going to your father's. Do remember to use your lotion if you visit the forge. Those flames will dry out your skin and give your wrinkles."

Eros rolled his eyes.

"And put oil in your hair. You don't want split ends. Your curls are too beautiful."

Again, Eros remained silent. He could hear the click-clacking of his mother's heels on the marble floor as she walked away and, for a moment, he considered asking if she and Ares would be up for a family dinner. It was late, though, by mortal standards, and Eros was tired. He let his eyes drift closed and soon slumber overtook him.

Chapter Six

The sun was barely above the horizon when Hephaestus awoke. He stretched and slipped out of bed, pulling on the same clothes he'd manifested when he'd fallen. Today he would buy more clothing and parts for the water heater. If Zion or Kiara woke up before he left, he could see about looking at the boy's bike too. Then he'd be able to get the parts needed for it, as well.

Surprisingly, Zion was already awake when Hephaestus wandered downstairs. The boy was sitting at the kitchen island, watching a couple of blue and beige dogs on his tablet while he ate brightly colored circles out of a bowl.

Milk dribbled down the boy's chin when he smiled at Hephaestus.

"Good morning," Hephaestus grunted, fighting a yawn.

"Morning," Zion greeted. "There's Fruit Loops in the cupboard if you want some. Mom's in the office, but she made coffee too." He frowned. "She says I can't have any."

"Smart woman. Coffee is a grown-up drink. It'll stunt your growth."

"What does stunt mean?" Zion asked.

"Hurt. Hinder. To stop or slow. Coffee will make it where you don't grow as tall," Hep replied

"Oh. My dad was tall. Mom says I'll be tall like him," Zion said.

"Probably. Most boys are close to their father's height," Hep said.

"Is your dad tall?" Zion asked.

Hephaestus chuckled as he opened cupboards, looking for a mug. He found one with a NASA symbol and filled it with the bitter black liquid simmering in a pot on the counter. "The tallest. When I was little, I thought he was a giant."

Zion giggled. "Giants aren't real."

"Oh?" Hephaestus raised a brow but continued to smile as he sipped at his coffee. "I think they are. There's lots of stories about them."

"Stories are fake. Like TV shows," Zion said.

"Not all of them are. Some are true, like the ones you learn in school," he replied.

Zion scrunched up his face. "Like the ones about sharks and space?"

Hephaestus nodded. "Yes, and some stories are so old that it's hard to know if they're true or not. A lot has happened on this little planet since its creation."

"What's your favorite story?" Zion asked.

The man thought for a moment. "When I was little, my dad used to tell me stories about him and his siblings. They were always my favorite. My grandparents weren't good people and my dad, and his siblings stopped them from doing something bad."

"Oh…" Zion stared down into his bowl of cereal. "I don't know my grandparents, but mom says they were good people."

"I'm sure they were," Hep replied.

Kiara entered the kitchen like a whirlwind. Her phone was wedged between her shoulder and ear as she waved around an empty coffee cup and a folded piece of paper. She bumped Zion's shoulder and smiled at him on her way to the coffee pot.

Reigning on Earth

"I have a new handy man," Kiara stated exasperatedly. "Just give me another month and we'll pass inspection. I swear… yes…yes…I know, Betsy. I know, just please talk to your husband, and convince him to hold off on the inspection for one month. That's all I need."

Hephaestus raised a brow and continued sipping from his own mug as Kiara filled hers.

"Thank you. I owe you. I'll bring a tray of cupcakes by this week as a gesture of goodwill," she gushed.

When she ended the call, Kiara slid her phone into her pocket and handed Hephaestus the paper she was carrying. "I need you to fill this out, ASAP."

He put the paper in his back pocket, promising to do as she requested. "Will do, boss. What's this about a month until inspection?"

She moaned, falling to lean against the counter next to him. The way she stared into her coffee mug was the way Hephaestus had seen voyagers stare at the temple of Delphi, like it was their last hope of happiness.

"The city's on my case about the disrepair of the house. They won't let me reopen the bed and breakfast unless I pass an inspection, which I failed last November and is why there's no one here." She bit her lip and groaned, "Well, one of the reasons. The rotting floor boards, and lack of hot water are two more. Speaking of which…"

"I'll have it up and running today," Hephaestus assured. He didn't know what compelled him to do so, but he nudged her shoulder with his own and gave her a smile he hadn't used since he'd first approached Aphrodite about marriage. It was a shy smile. A meek and reserved smile. A smile that hinted at his vulnerable side and how much he yearned to share it with

The Fall of Fire

another being. "We've got this. Come inspection time, this Betsy and husband won't recognize the place."

"It's only a month," she lamented. "How are we supposed to get everything fixed in that short of time? There's so much to do?"

If Hephaestus had his cyclops workers, the home would be renovated overnight. If he used his magick, it could be fixed with a mere snap of his hands, but he was never one to take the easy way out. What many people didn't realize was that he wasn't just the god of forges. He was the god of creativity and like with any creative work, the process was as important as the final piece. Apollo understood this, but most of the other Olympians did not. Still, even without his abilities and cyclops, if he didn't sleep, he'd be able to repair the home more than enough to pass inspection. The trick would be doing it in a way that Kiara wouldn't notice his lack of human qualities.

"I can help," Zion chimed in.

Hephaestus chuckled and Kiara gave her son a fond smile.

"Thank you, sweetie, but these are big boy projects," she told Zion.

"I'm a big boy," the child defended.

"In ancient Greece, he'd nearly be a man," Hephaestus winked at the kid. "I wouldn't mind the help. If he wants to be an engineer when he grows up, he'll need to learn some of the basic skills first. I can teach him if you're okay with it."

Kiara blinked. "Really? You'd do that?"

"Sure. I tried to teach my stepson, once, but he's not really a grease monkey," Hep replied.

"Oh?" Kiara asked.

"He's more of a suit and tie kind of guy. His mother's work, I'm afraid," He told her.

"Please, mom," Zion begged. "I promise I won't get in his way."

"I..," she sighed. With a curious glance at Hephaestus, she asked, "You're sure?"

"Completely," the god grinned. "Don't worry. The kid will be safe with me."

"For some reason," she spoke slowly, "I have no doubt about that. I don't know what it is, Hep, but something tells me I can trust you…and I don't trust anyone. Especially not with my son."

Chapter Seven

Time in Olympus worked differently than the human realm. Day and night only occurred because the gods willed it to. Otherwise, time was basically nonexistent. They could operate both in and outside of time whenever they pleased, which was why Eros was slightly confused to notice he'd woken up so late. He should have automatically woken up when he wanted to, which was when the light was still young, but he woke up in the evening with a dry mouth and a deep tiredness nestled in his bones. What was this? Gods didn't get tired. There was no reason he should have felt this way.

On top of the sleepiness, the house was too cold. He shivered as he stood. Hephaestus's forge should be keeping the establishment well heated. Normally the marble floor would be comfortably warm beneath his feet, but he flinched when his bare toes met with chilled stone.

Thunder rumbled and, for a moment, the mount shook. He stumbled into the wall and gripped the engraved cherubs with all his might. A thin crack spread along the ceiling, causing him to gasp. Outside his home, through the glassless window of his room, he could hear the other Olympians freaking out. Zeus was yelling, his voice booming like the storms he commanded.

With a creased brow, Eros righted himself once the tremor stopped and rushed towards the forges. Earthquakes never happened on the mount, and he'd hate to think what one could mean for his stepfather's forge, which was built into Mountain Olympus's very core.

A staircase was built into the Aphrodite-Hephaestus house that led into the forges. It started out sleek with marble steps and gold trimming but gradually turned into rocks and clay. The intricate scones turned into candles set into crevices of the wall and the sturdy railing turned into a mounted pipe.

The sounds of clanging weren't the symphony they usually were and even here, deep beneath the mount, the air was too cold.

"Hephaestus?" Eros called out, winding his way through the caverns of the forge. He knew the path by heart only because of pestering his stepfather when he was a child.

The center of the forge is a circular area with stalactites hanging from the ceiling. The cyclopes worked in their own separate part of the forges, while the center forge supplied the heat and power for its connected counterparts. Hephaestus was the only being who worked at the center forge. It was the first forge of Olympus, born with Hephaestus, and was maintained by the god's presence.

Eros could hear the dissatisfied grunts of the cyclopes. They were muttering to each other, and the young god didn't need to understand their native tongue to know it was about the emptiness he found in the center forge.

Hephaestus's work bench was cluttered with projects. A

scroll of orders was unwound on a stand by the bench, but the god of the forge was nowhere to be seen. Thick shadows flickered across the cavern from the dying embers in the forge.

Eros's heart stopped.

Hephaestus's hammer was gone. The forge's flames were dying and there, sitting on the bench with a note taped to it, was Eros's bow. With shaky fingers, he unfolded the note and nearly crumpled like the paper in his hands when he read, "The forges are no more".

In a broken voice, the boy yelled out for his stepfather.

Chapter Eight

Hephaestus was in the shed, looking over Zion's bike when he felt it. He stumbled backwards as Eros's voice shook his core. Like all gods, he could feel when he was called upon, but he could not remember a time when someone had prayed his name in such a broken way. He could feel Eros's pain. The boy's feelings of neglect and shock flooded him. It took him a moment to steady himself against the rickety wall of the shed.

"Hep?" Zion asked from where he was knelt by his bike. "You okay?"

Hephaestus waited a moment for the prayer to pass. He had a feeling it'd be Eros who discovered his absence and expected the boy to be shocked, but the full onslaught of his stepson's feelings was stronger than he'd imagined. For a moment, he wished the boy would continue his prayer to give him some kind of insight into whether he'd found his bow and the note Hephaestus had left him or if he was in some kind of physical turmoil that he needed aid with. However, the prayer was only his name, and it remained that way, reverberating off the walls of his mortal flesh.

Once the wave died down enough that he could breathe, Hephaestus pushed away from the wall and assured the child in front of him, "I'm alright, Zion. Just a little heartburn."

Zion accepted his answer like only a child would and bounced up, almost knocking over his bike. "Okay. Can we go to the store now?"

"Yeah," Hephaestus shook himself, trying to dispel the lingering bits of Eros's prayer. "Yeah, let's go."

The hardware store wasn't too far away but Kiara had told Hephaestus to take her car. He'd never driven a vehicle before but was sure he could handle the machine. Zion strapped himself into the backseat while Hephaestus buckled himself into the driver's chair. The car was a stick shift, not the automatic he'd been hoping for.

While Zion was busy adjusting his twisted strap, Hephaestus touched the gearshift, letting a spark of his abilities flow through the machine. The car came to life beneath his fingers and told him everything he needed to know about driving it. His shoulders straightened and he turned to look behind him as he backed the car out of the driveway like he had the license humans required to operate their vehicles. For a moment he wondered how Kiara would feel about having lent him her car once she read the document he'd filled out for that morning. After all, she'd soon learn that not only did he not possess a driver's license, he also didn't have a birth certificate or any form of identification.

The man at the hardware store was helpful and Hephaestus and Zion soon had everything on their list. They picked up some extra items, such as lumber (which Hephaestus strapped on top of the car), paint, varnish, and nails, and then stopped

Reigning on Earth

by the diner to grab lunch.

With three orders of BLTs and lemonades in hand, the duo made their way back home to eat with Kiara, who they pried out of her office.

After lunch, Kiara once again disappeared behind her desk while Hephaestus and Zion ventured down into the basement to fix the water heater. Zion turned out to be a better study than Eros but he chattered just as much. He asked questions about everything and told Hephaestus about his school, friends, and summer plans.

"Will you take me fishing?" he asked after nearly an hour of rambling while helping Hephaestus change out the water heater's parts.

Hephaestus wiped his hands on a rag and chuckled. "I've never been, but I wouldn't mind trying."

The boy beamed. "My dad and I used to go fishing all the time before he died. I can teach you."

Hephaestus's brow furrowed. "Maybe you should ask your mom to take you instead. I don't want to encroach on a tradition."

Zion blinked. "I don't know what that means. Mom hates fishing. She won't take me. But she likes camping. Maybe we could all go camping together and you and I can catch fish to eat."

"That would be fun," Hephaestus stated honestly. A family vacation…even if he wasn't technically part of Zion and Kiara's little family, the thought sounded like a fairy tale to him.

After tackling the water heater, the duo fixed Zion's bike, cleaned up the front flower beds, and located the rotting floorboards. Hephaestus would fix the floorboards while Zion and his mom slept, but he let the boy mark them with a

The Fall of Fire

permanent marker and help him pre-cut the boards.

While he worked quietly on the floorboards, the home shuttered as the earth shifted. He frowned and went to the window to look towards his home. The skies were gray with thick, wooly clouds, but the storm didn't look otherworldly. There was a static in the air, however, that picked at his hairy arms, and he could have sworn that he heard the ground itself groan.

Chapter Nine

Kiara stared at computer screen in confusion. This was impossible. How could a man simply not exist? Yet, there, on the screen was the background check she'd ran on Hep and in big bold letters it declared, "no results found".

"What the hell," she said to the empty office. She refreshed the page but the results were the same. Perhaps she entered something wrong?

Name: Hephaestus F. Olympian

Ethnicity: Greek

Parents: Z and Hera Olympian

Emergency Contact: None

Previous address: Athens, Greece

Work Experience: Trade work, blacksmithing, mechanics, and engineering.

Half of the form was left blank, which Kiara had somewhat expected from the nomadic man, but her search still should have brought up something. The government website was insistent that Hep didn't exist, though.

"Okay," she took a breath to clear her mind. "Let's try something else."

Google, after all, was a woman's best friend. She entered Hephaestus's info and blinked when the screen instantly filled with results. Article after article showed up regarding the Greek god Hephaestus, his temple in Athens, and his linage.

Her eyes narrowed as she clicked on the first result and read, "Hephaestus was a god worshiped in ancient Greece. He was most known as the god of the forge, fire, and creativity. According to myth, Hephaestus was the son of the goddess Hera. Some scholars speculate that his father was Zeus, but many myths indicate Hera used magic to conceive him to get revenge on Zeus for doing likewise with another child. When he was born, he was deformed, leading Hera to cast him from Mount Olympus. Later, Zeus also cast the god from the mount."

Kiara found herself falling through a rabbit hole as she read each article. Hephaestus, or Hephaistos, as some of the writers referred to him was often depicted with dark curls and a hammer. He was usually near and anvil and dressed in dirty bronze or red robes. Her frown deepened when she stumbled on a statue of the mythical god who looked almost exactly like her handy man. The statue's beard was unkept but thick, it's curls were grown out, falling on his shoulders, like Hep's would if he didn't constantly pull it back into a holder.

Though the statues showed the god's torso to be muscular and thick, one of its feet and legs were deformed. A deformity like that would not lead to tragic end, but it would cause pain while walking and, perhaps, require a brace such as the one Hep wore.

Leaning back in her chair, Kiara shook her head. What was she thinking? How could the man who she'd found wandering the highway be an ancient and powerful god? Greek mythology was just that, right? It was myths. A dying religion. Surely it wasn't real…but…then again…he looked so much like that statue.

Clicking out of the tab, she opened her email. Kiara wasn't going to consider Hep was an ancient deity until she's checked with all her sources, which meant emailing the local police department where her friend Travis worked.

Hey, Travis,

Weird question. I have a new employee and every background check I've ran on him came back inconclusive. I was wondering if you could work your magic and see what you can dig up. I'd hate to be living with a serial killer. He seems normal but he didn't have any documentation on him. He's a nomad, I think. Here's what he gave me to go off.

Thanks,

Kiara Smith

She attached a copy of Hep's info and sent the email. Travis the chief of police was a busy man but she'd used his work email, which he checked as frequently as possible. She'd likely have a reply within twenty-four hours. Until then…she clicked back to the tab about the legends of Hephaestus.

Chapter Ten

Eros sprinted up the steps of Mount Olympus, towards the throne room located at the peak. Zeus had called an emergency meeting of the gods as Olympus continued to be rocked by quakes. Eros hadn't yet informed anyone of his stepfather's disappearance but would need to soon. The problem was, he didn't know who to tell and, even then, he had very little to tell them. He knew nothing except that the god had left. He didn't know why or how long ago.

"Order!" Zeus was yelling, banging his fist against the arm of his throne like a gavel.

Eros stumbled into the throne room and tried to be an inconspicuous as possible as he slipped into his throne, which was directly between the thrones of his parents. Aphrodite and Ares were already seated, as were the rest of their kin. Eros was the last to arrive. Not counting Hephaestus, who's metal throne remained empty as Zeus began.

"I said order!" The gossiping fell into a silence and Zeus continued, "Can someone tell me what in Styx is going on? Hades? Poseidon?"

"The oceanic volcanos have suddenly become active," Poseidon stated, stroking his long beard. "Triton has dived into the depths and discovered a stirring in the tomb of Oceanus."

"The gates of Lapetus's prison are shuttering," Hades added. "The rivers of Tartarus are running unusually hot. I keep them boiling, but they are turning to steam."

"I sent Nike to Pallus's grave, and she found it empty," Ares remarked.

Zeus cursed. "Oceanus, Lapetus, Pallus…Has anyone checked on father?"

Eros's grandparents and their siblings were quiet. Eventually, Hades spoke up and stated, "Cronus cannot awaken on his own. We made sure of that."

"We cut him to shreds," Poseidon angered, "and buried him deep inside the inner workings of the realms. It would take the magic of Hecate and each of the six divine weapons to resurrect him."

Zeus nodded. "But the titans are waking. If they destroy Olympus and take our weapons, they could bring back our parents."

The Fall of Fire

"And then all of the realms would be doomed," Hera sighed beside her husband. "Perhaps we should reach out to other deity realms. The Norse, Egyptian, Indian, or Christian realms may assist us."

Zeus growled. "We will not contact them. We don't need…"

"Hera has a point," Athena, the goddess of battle strategy, interrupted her father. "You're disdain for the other deities is not unreciprocated by the council, but the original six barley defeated the titans in the first war. If a second war commences and Cronus's followers decide to seek retribution and resurrection for their kin, we will need all the fire power we can get."

"My sister is correct." Ares was lounging in his throne wearing a leather jacket and heavy boots, looking like he didn't have a care in the world, but when he spoke everyone listened. Athena nodded her respect to him, acknowledging his acknowledgement of her wisdom. "If it comes to war, we will need more than Nike, Athena, and myself to defeat the titans."

"You're saying your armies aren't strong enough?" Zeus sneered.

"I'm saying that thousands of years in impressment and death can make a being cranky and we can't overlook the fact that a pissed off titan is good for no one. They are stronger than us. They came before all of creation. With humanity's faith in us dwindling by the century, our powers grow weaker, and we cannot take on a fully charged titan. They don't draw on prayers and belief to maintain themselves, they merely are."

"Yahweh is the closet thing we have to a titan…" Athena proceeded.

"No!" Zeus crossed his arms like a petulant toddler. "We will handle this ourselves. You don't see Odin coming to us in fear of Fenrir or Yahweh coming to us because of Lucifer. We will not go to them for assistance."

"Then what do you suggest?" Athena challenged.

"Ares and I have already discussed with Hephaestus the rearming of his troops. We will do the same with yours and Nikes, plus maintain the divine weapons. Hephaestus!" Zeus turned to order and visibly flinched when he noticed the empty throne. "Hermes, I told you to message everyone about the meeting."

"I did," Hermes frowned. "I sent a direct message to the forge."

"If you sent it to the forge instead of Hephaestus, himself, he didn't get it," Eros spoke up for the first time since entering the throne room. It was such a rare occasion for a minor god or goddess to speak in the council meetings that everyone present gave him a skeptical look.

"What are you talking about?" Ares raised a brow.

"I went to the forge after I came home." Eros took a breath to still himself. "Hephaestus is not there, and the forges have cooled."

"Th-that's impossible," Zeus stuttered. "Ares has an order of equipment due tomorrow."

Ares frowned. "He was pissed about that order."

"He's always upset," Zeus stated venomously. "It means nothing."

"I wonder where he got that trait from," Hera sneered.

"There's no proof that he is my son."

"I'm not like you," Hera scoffed. "I don't cheat on my spouse. He is absolutely your son."

Ares and Aphrodite shared a look. In unison, they leaned towards their son and Ares whispered, "You are sure the forges are cold?"

The Fall of Fire

"Yes," Eros whispered back. "Even the house is cold."

Aphrodite sighed, pinching the bridge of her elegant nose. "I told you I should have stopped by the forge before going to your home."

"I didn't tell you not to," Ares reminded. "You're the one that said it'd make us late to our reservations at Demeter's."

She glared at her lover. "Don't. This is not the time."

"Of course, it's not," he smirked. "It's never the time You can't keep doing this, Dite."

"Me? You're the one that uses him as your personal blacksmith."

"You're never in his bed."

"You'd rather I be in his than yours?"

"I'd rather you choose so I don't feel like I'm stealing my brother's wife every time she comes home." Ares sighed, noticing that he'd risen his voice and the other Olympians were now watching his family. "Never mind, you're right. This isn't the time."

"Agreed," Zeus stated. "Your spat can wait until it's behind closed doors. For now, we need to find Hephaestus so he can provide for our legions. Hermes?"

"Yes, my lord?"

"I want him found. Immediately."

"Yes, my lord."

Eros watched as Ares frowned. Behind his sunglasses, the god of war was clearly displeased.

Chapter Eleven

"That should do it," Hephaestus stated with a smile, descending the ladder he'd used to change a bulb in the kitchen.

"Thank you," Kiara stated. "You're a godsend. I swear."

Hephaestus chuckled. "Trust me, my lady, I wasn't sent here by any god."

Kiara hummed. It'd been nearly a week since she sent Hep's info to Travis, who told her he needed to do some more digging before he shared his findings with her. After the weekend, she was sure he didn't have any findings to share. Nothing about Hephaestus's info added up. Her own searching only pulled up even more articles about Greek mythology and religions. She'd been saying things to try and get a reaction out of the handy man since the background check came back inconclusive.

So far, he hadn't said anything that hinted at him being a god. There were times, however, when he said things like "I wasn't sent here by any god" and it gave her the impression that he was speaking from personal experience. It was weird and she was starting to wonder if she was dreaming. Maybe she'd fallen asleep reading a YA book and her mind created Hephaestus. If that were so, she'd hate to think about what her brain was trying to tell her with the dream.

It'd been a year since Simon died and she was reluctant to get back into the dating scene. People told her that she should dress up and go out with one of the local men who'd asked her out, for Zion's sake, but she didn't see how replacing his father would be good for either of them. Simon was a good man, and no one could truly replace him. He and Kiara had met in college and moved to Lexington after graduation, when he was accepted for a job at the fire station.

Zion was born in Lexington and Simon steadily worked up the ranks. He hoped to be fire chief some day and had put his name in the running when his chief announced his retirement. Sadly, Simon never got to see his dream come true as he died

The Fall of Fire

in a fire only a week after formally accepting the new position.

Since his death, Kiara had remained independent. She had no family in town. Her parents had died when she was young and she'd bounced around from one foster family to the next, never finding one that she meshed with. Simon's parents had accepted her as part of their family, but his father passed away from cancer only two years after their wedding and his mother ended up dying suddenly in her sleep only a couple months later. Simon said she died from heartbreak, but the official diagnoses was that she simply stopped breathing.

Being a single mother wasn't a bad life. Sure, there were some people who looked at her like she was trash but most of them were outsiders. The townspeople, themselves, loved her and she'd found support in an elderly woman who ran the generation center. Auntie Hestie, as she liked to be called, adopted the single mothers, the single fathers, the children with bad home lives, and the older people whose family never came to visit. She loved everyone and was always willing to sit down and chat about life over a cup of coffee.

Kiara stared down at the box of lightbulbs in her hands, wondering what advice Auntie Hestie would give her about Hep. For an unexplainable reason, she felt drawn to him. For the first time in her life she wanted to break tradition and ask him out, but how would he respond and was it even a good idea since she was his employer?

She huffed, earning a raised brow from Hep, who was closing the ladder.

"You okay?" he asked.

"Yeah, I'm fine," she said.

He nodded and didn't push her, though she was certain her internal struggle was obvious.

Reigning on Earth

"Okay. I finished the floorboards last night. They're stained to match the original wood and varnished to last. When you get a chance, I'd like to run some ideas by you for the rooms. I think a coat of paint would brighten things up and I can refurbish the furniture already in the rooms. It'll make them feel newer."

Her nose scrunched up and Hephaestus kept his thoughts of how cute it was to himself. "You finished all the floorboards? Already? It's only been a week since you started them. How did you…"

"Don't question it," he grinned. With a shrug he added, "I'm good with my hands."

Her face heated at the implications of his words. Was he flirting with her?

He winked, plucking the lightbulb box out of her hands.

"I…uh…," she cleared her throat. "Paint sounds good. Yellow is cheery."

"I was thinking of themes. You could call them the blue room, yellow room, pink room. Paint them to match the color and get matching bedding."

"That's…That's a good idea. We have five guest rooms, though. We'll need two more colors."

"Green and purple?" he asked.

"I like those," she said.

"I can go to Harvey's today and get the paint," he told her.

"I'll come with. I feel like you've been doing so much around here. I'd like to help," she said,.

He chuckled. "It's my job, but you and Zion are always welcome to help. I like the company."

"Great," she shyly bit her lip.

Without thinking, Hep reached out and thumbed her lip from between her teeth. He ran his thumb across her lower lip and her breath caught. "You should stop biting your lip. You're going to hurt it."

She didn't know what to say. Her eyes locked with his and her chest tightened. She couldn't breathe.

Hep tilted his head, searching her eyes with his own, and brought his hand down to tip her chin towards him. He swayed forward and she barely realized she did the same. They were going to kiss, and she was okay with that. She wanted to know how his chapped lips felt beneath her own, but then Zion bounded into the kitchen.

"I need a Band-Aid!" the boy exclaimed, forcing Hep and Kiara back into reality. They separated, shaking off the moment. He went to put away the ladder and lightbulbs and she retrieved a first aid kit.

When Hephaestus returned to the kitchen, Kiara was placing a kiss on top of the space themed bandage on Zion's knee.

"There you go, sweetie," she cooed. "All better."

"Thanks, mom!" Zion hopped off the counter.

"Go get in the car," Kiara told him. "We're going to go to the store with Hep and pick out paint for the guest rooms. Then I thought we'd swing by the Generation Center, since they're having a garage sale today." She glanced at Hep. "Maybe we'll find something that'll look good in one of the rooms."

"Sounds like a plan," Hep agreed with a smile.

Picking out paint turned out to be the easy part. Finding the correct equipment to paint the ceiling of the rooms was a little hard, but nothing was as difficult as making their way through the crowds at the Generation Center.

The Generation Center was packed with Lexington's occupants and visitors from out of town. The center's building was a brick rectangle with limited landscaping and a cracked parking lot. The floor had beige tiles and the walls were off white. The large, floor to ceiling windows made the space feel roomier than it was.

For the garage sale a cloth was draped over the center's salad bar and the tables were arranged in rows. Various items littered the tables while paintings, tools, electronics, and other big items were aligned along the walls. Near the front of the room, the high school cheerleaders were selling baked goods to raise money for new uniforms while a boy scout troop volunteered to help people carry their purchases to their vehicles.

A sign on the front door stated that all items were freewill donations and that funds would go towards the upkeep of the center. Hephaestus noted a rack of men's clothing in the back and beelines for it. He spotted several flannel and plaid shirts that he liked, a couple of Henley's, jeans, and belts. Zion was knelt beside him, looking at a pair of roller blades.

"Those are too big for you," Hep pointed out. "Go look at the kid's rack."

"Okay," Zion stepped around Hep to look at the rack two over from him. The man could still see the boy in his peripheral vision and kept a close eye on him while he wandered the sale. A hammer necklace caught his eye and he stopped to admire it. It was bronze and shaped like his own hammer instead of Thor's. He added the necklace to his purchases and accepted a bag from a boy scout when it was offered to him to make his shopping easier.

Kiara was over by the furniture and called out for Hep. She had her hands on her hips and was staring into an ornate wooden framed mirror when he scooted beside her.

"How hard do you think it'd be to sand this mirror down and repaint it?" she asked him.

Hep took a closer look at the mirror. The paint on it was already pealing and the frame was cracked in few places, making the glass unstable.

"It wouldn't be too hard. We'd need to sand it and get some wood glue to repair the frame. Then we could paint and mount it."

She gestured towards a nearby dresser. "It matches that dresser. Think we could do both?"

"That dresser's in pretty good condition. It could use a fresh coat of paint and we could change out the knobs to give it a more modern look, but otherwise it's a simple clean up. You thinking for a guest room?"

She nodded.

"They won't fit in the car. Do you know someone who'd let us borrow a truck?" Hep asked.

"I think so. Let me call Betsy real quick and see if Noah would let us use his," she said.

"Okay. I'm going to go check out the bathroom accessories for any towel racks for the guest baths."

Kiara was on the phone with Betsy, arranging to borrow her husband's truck when Travis and his wife entered the center. The chief of police immediately spotted her and told his wife to give him a moment. While his wife went to peruse the sale, he approached Kiara and waited patiently for her to end her call.

"I'm glad to see you here," he stated. "I've been meaning to email you."

"It's alright," she glanced around, locating Hep across the room. "Should we step outside and talk?"

"I think that'd be a good idea. That the guy?" he asked, gesturing towards Hep before they walked outside, where they had more privacy.

"Yeah," she replied.

"What made you think inviting a stranger into your home was a good idea?" Travis asked.

"I don't know. He seems nice. I was reluctant at first, but he's only been with us for a week, and he's already helped us out a lot. Please tell me you didn't find out he's a murderer?" She asked.

"I didn't find anything," Travis admitted. "According to my search, he doesn't exist."

"That's impossible. He's right inside," she asked.

Travis took a deep breath and held his tongue as a group of people walked past them. He nodded at the people greeting as they went inside the center. Once they were gone, he leaned closer to Kiara and whispered, "I haven't seen anything like this before. He has no birth records, driving history, felony history…I can't find his name mentioned anywhere."

Now Kiara knew that wasn't true. A Google search would have led the cop to stories about the Greek god her handy man shared a name with.

"Look, I do have one lead on him, but it's loose," Travis stated.

"What do you mean?" She asked.

"His last name is the same as Auntie Hesti's. Maybe they're related. She's always said she moved here to put distance between herself and her family. Maybe he's a relative," Travis said.

"Her last name is Olympian?" She asked.

He nodded. "Her legal name is Hestia Olympian."

"Okay. Thanks, Travis. I'll talk to her," she told him. "Hey," he caught her arm when she went to go back inside. "Listen, be careful. Okay? We don't know anything about this guy. If you want, I can get him a room at the motel until we figure this out, that way he's not around you or Zion any more than he needs to be."

"He's not a criminal," Kiara stated.

"You don't know that," Travis replied.

"I don't, but I feel like I do. I appreciate the offer, Travis, but I think if he was going to hurt us, he would have already. He's had plenty of chances. Honestly, I think he's just a guy who's looking for a place to belong," she said.

Chapter Twelve

Auntie Hesti was Lexington's token maiden aunt, though she wasn't truly an aunt to anyone in town. She was an older lady with curls that magically maintained their red hue, despite her age. Her skin was soft, fluffy, and her frame was small. She'd been part of the community for over thirty years and kept a modest residence near the hospital. She was friendly to everyone and cared about the community as if she were born and raised there.

Five years ago, Hesti took over the Generation Center when the former coordinator left to pursue a career elsewhere. There were talks from the city about shutting the center down when no applicants had come in for the open job, but Hesti couldn't let that happen. The community needed a place where all the generations felt welcome. A place that could be used for birthdays, graduations, garage sales, and a place that regularly served meals to the senior community members. So, she stepped up and took over the center, keeping everything much the same as it had been before her.

She had exited the kitchen of the center with a plate of freshly baked cookies for the cheerleaders to sell when she spotted the

Reigning on Earth

last person, she thought she'd ever seen in Lexington. Her nephew was admiring a sturdy, wooden towel rod and her brother's orders rang through her mind.

"Find Hephaestus!" Zeus had ordered at the council meeting. Of course, the order had been given to Hermes, not Hestia, who had no desire to be involved in her family's drama.

Hephaestus had always been the odd duck of the group. She remembered when he was born with a deformed foot and lazy eyes. Hera threw a temper tantrum that her son wasn't perfect and then threw him off Mount Olympus. To that day, Hestia still didn't know what Hera had hoped to accomplish by the action since she'd know the fall wouldn't kill the child.

Baby Hephaestus had landed in Greece and Hestia had gone to his rescue. He'd been crying when she'd arrived and she'd wrapped him in her warm, red cloak, tucking him close to her body. For years she'd raised him in secret, letting the humans believe he was her son. His mortal form didn't look much like hers, but no one questioned his parentage. Once Hera had calmed down after three years, Hestia returned the child to his parents. Some days she wished she hadn't.

Like Hephaestus, Hestia had always felt out of place in their family. She was a goddess of eternal maidenhood, so she didn't marry or have children of her own. Her siblings, the original Greek gods, left her to her own devices after they destroyed their parents. Hades was cast into the Underworld, Zeus declared himself king, Poseidon made a home for himself in oceans of the mortal realm, Demeter had her daughter Persephone, and Hera married Zeus.

Though Hestia had a home on Mount Olympus, she was rarely there. She preferred living among humans. Every sixty or so years she would switch locations, telling the friends she'd

The Fall of Fire

made that she was moving closer to family. Despite being the goddess of home, hearth, and hospitality, her family wasn't someone she saw often, and it didn't bother her, usually. She was independent, as the first goddess to choose eternal maidenhood, and was the aunt her siblings, nieces, and nephews, dropped their kids off with when they'd run out of patience with them. Since a new god hadn't been born in centuries, she'd remained away from her family.

When Zeus ordered Hephaestus to be found, she'd had no plans to help Hermes. If Hephaestus had finally escaped their family, then good for him. She was proud of him, truly, for their family was the very definition of dysfunctional. Still, she could not simply ignore the god of the forge when he was in her town.

With her mind made up, she took a deep breath to calm the storm inside of her and approached her nephew with a warm smile. She wondered if he'd recognize her as an old woman. The mortal form she habitually took around him was a much younger one.

"Hephaestus," Hestia greeted. Her voice was smooth like honey and warm like freshly brewed tea.

When he turned to look at her, the confusion in his eyes gave way to recognition. "Hestia?"

She gave him a once over, taking in his dusty clothing and pulled back hair. His beard looked kept, which was a nice change for him, and dirt was caked under his nails. He looked much the same as he always had. Black hair, deep brown eyes, and bronze skin stretched over the muscles of a blacksmith. The stench of sweat that she was used to smelling on him was gone, however, and the worry lines around his mouth had vanished.

Her shoulders relaxed and she reached out, drawing her nephew into a hug. "Hephaestus. You've had us all worried."

He snorted. "I doubt that."

She hummed. "Well, you had a few of us worried. Eros is beside himself."

Hephaestus' face turned sour. "He's a grown god. He'll be fine."

"I have no doubt of that. You helped raise him and any child you had a hand in rearing is sure to be a survivor. However, we do need to talk." She glanced around at their surroundings. "Somewhere more private. I have a quaint residence by the hospital. You cannot miss it. It's a deep navy with red shutters and the most beautiful garden. Come by and see me."

He rubbed the back of his neck. "If you're going to try to talk me into going home, you'll be wasting your time."

She smiled a secretive smile and waved at Kiara and Travis, who came through the generation center's doors. She'd know the instant she'd saw Hephaestus that Mount Olympus was no longer his home, so as the chief of police and bed and breakfast owner approached them, she stated, "How could I talk you into going home when you are already there?"

"Kiara!" the redhead drew the other woman into a hug. "It's wonderful to see you. I was just catching up with Hephaestus."

"You know Hep?" Kiara asked at the same time Travis asked, "You know him?"

"Of course, I do," Hestia grinned. "He is my nephew."

"Oh," Kiara beamed. "That's great. I mean…I didn't know he had family in town." She gave Hephaestus a faux glare. "You could have told me. It would have made the background check unnecessary. Instead, I had to get Travis working on it."

"Oh dear," Hestia sighed. "Don't tell me you left your

The Fall of Fire

documentation at home, nephew of mine."

"I...Uh...," Hep didn't know what to say.

"Hep used to live with me when he was a child," Hestia stated to Kiara and Travis. "I'm sure I have copies of his documents if you need them."

"Please," Travis started but was interrupted by Kiara who said, "That won't be needed."

"It won't?" Travis raised a brow.

"It won't," Kiara assured. "We know Auntie Hesti. If she says Hep is family, then I believe her. And I'm sure she would tell me if I was harboring a criminal."

Hestia laughed. "He's no criminal. In fact, you can't get any further away from being one than him. Hep, why didn't you tell me you were coming to town and, am I to assume you are the new handy man everyone is saying Kiara has?"

"Um," again Hep was at a loss for words.

"No matter," Hestia waved his stammer away. "You could have stayed with me, but I see you are in good hands. There is no one in town you'd be better off with than our dear Kiara and god know she could use a...man...of your skills."

Travis had his arms crossed and was glaring at Hephaestus suspiciously. Hestia patted his arm. "Relax, chief. He's as gentle and gentle comes."

Travis dropped his arms and shook his head in defeat. "If you say so. I better get back to my wife." He tipped his hat. "Ladies. Hep."

"So," Kiara looked between the Olympian duo with her hands on her hips, "is Hesti short for Hestia?"

Hep choked on air.

Hestia grinned. "It certainly is. You were always a smart one. I invited Hephaestus over for dinner tonight. Why don't you join us? And bring your child. I'd love to chat with the three of you without having to worry about the Bettys of the barbershop hearing anything."

"She…" Hep began.

Kiara cut him off with, "We'd love to. We'll see you tonight. What time would you like us over?"

Hestia hummed. "Let's say seven. I'll cook up something special. Have you ever had lamb?"

"I haven't," Kiara admitted.

"You'll love it. It's tender. Until then, I suppose," Hestia waved at another group of people arriving for the generation center's sale, "I'll see you two later."

The moment Hestia left it felt like a weight was lifted off Hep's chest and he could breathe again. He wanted to curse at the skies. His aunt knew he was in town. Would she tell his father? Would she help Hermes find him?

Kiara was watching him curiously. "I think we should check out and head home. We need to talk."

He nodded, swallowing around a lump of dread. She'd known who Hestia was, so it only reasoned that she'd figured out who he was too and that thought scared him more than anything.

Chapter Thirteen

"I need you to be completely honest with me," Kiara said, shutting the door to a guest room behind her and Hep so Zion wouldn't interrupt them. "I ran your information through an online background check and contacted the chief of police to do a check of his own. Everything I found says you don't exist."

Hep leaned against the window, gripping the ledge tightly. His lips were pressed into a thin line and his eyebrows were scrunched. He looked like it physically pained him to speak. "I...I want to tell you...but you'll think I'm crazy."

"I already think I'm going crazy even considering what I am. Hep," she thrust her hands into the air exasperatedly. "I'm legit considering that you might be a Greek god."

Hep was silent. Kiara fell onto the old bed, which creaked.

"Hep," she prompted. "Please. I need the truth. I won't judge you."

He chuckled humorlessly. "Judging is the job of the gods, yet I would bring the wrath of fire down upon anyone who dared judge you."

Her forehead creased. "What are you saying?"

"I...," he took a deep breath. "I am Hephaestus. God of blacksmiths, forges, craftsmen, and creativity. I know this must sound insane to you, for the mortal realm has forgotten us, but it is my truth."

She took a deep, steadying breath. Surprisingly, she did not react other than to slowly stand and approach Hep like he was deer. "So...Hestia..."

"She is my aunt. The goddess of home, hearth, and hospitality. She's the eldest of the original six. The first child of Cronus and Rhea."

Kiara nodded. "Okay." She took another breath. "Okay. Listen, I'm not going to pretend that this doesn't freak me out a bit. I've read stories of Greek myths, but to accept that they are real..."

His eyes turned pleading. "I can leave if you want, but I love this job and I've felt more at home with you and Zion this last week than I have at any point in my existence. I like you, Kiara. I can't explain it, but I want to help you. To protect you and, if you'd let me, court you."

She snorted. "Court? Really?"

"What? Is that not the right word?" He asked.

"Courting is a little old school, don't you think?" She asked.

He shifted, looking at her bashfully. "I haven't been around the modern world in a long time. I'm sorry."

She smiled. "It's okay. I'll admit, I've found you attractive since you rescued me on the side of the road. You're just…I guess godly."

It was his turn to chortle as he shook his head. "No. Styx, no, don't say that. I'm no prince charming and I'm hardly a god. All I did in Olympus was forge weapons for my kin. Truthfully, I was merely a tool myself. "

"I don't see you as one," she said.

"I know. That's part of the reason I was drawn to you, I think. You're strong, smart, beautiful, and even though you need my help you don't treat me like I'm a servant," he told her.

"Because you're not. You're a human being…well, I guess you're not, but the sentiment remains. I see you as a person. You're more than just a handy man, Hep, and as far as 'courting' goes, I wouldn't say no to a date," she told him.

His eyes lit up like sunshine in a pool of honey. "Really?"

She shrugged. "Yeah. After Simon, I didn't think I'd date again, then you showed up and you immediately took to helping Zion and me. We…I…I can't explain what that means to me and even though I thought you were hot when you changed my tire your attractiveness increased ten-fold when I saw who you are with my son."

He stroked her face with his knuckles. "If I didn't think my wife would curse you, I'd say you are more beautiful than Aphrodite."

Kiara rolled her eyes and pushed Hep's hand away. "Please

don't. I've heard the stories. She's a jealous lover for someone who doesn't truly love you."

He sighed, "You have no idea."

Chapter Fourteen

Eros was beside himself. He felt like a child, sitting on his dad's sofa while his parents argued about what to do concerning his missing stepfather. Hermes was officially on the case, by order of Zeus, but he hadn't left Olympus yet. Which told Eros that Hermes couldn't find Hephaestus's power signature, which means the god of the forge must have invented something to shield him from his kin.

"Dite," Ares was in Aphrodite's face, pointing a finger at her, "this needs to end. I know everyone sees me as the bull-headed, younger version of my father, but I'm a better man than he ever was. I never should have kept seeing you when you married my brother."

"Oh, please," she sneered. "Our affair was just part of the iceberg. You, your father, and everyone else on Olympus treated Hephaestus like he was no better than a hammer. He's nothing but a tool in your belt."

Ares's laugh was loud, deep, and dry. "I protected him. I'm the only reason he lived here. Mother and father wanted him gone. A disabled god? Absurd! Athena and I were the ones who suggested a forge. We gave him a place to live."

"You gave him a prison!" Aphrodite yelled.

"Stop!" Eros interrupted. "This isn't helping. It doesn't matter why he left, anymore. We can cross that bridge once we find him."

Aphrodite threw her hands in the air. "And how are we

supposed to do that? If Hermes can't find him, then no one can."

"That's not completely true," Ares grunted, falling into a leather chair. "Hermes tracks power signatures. Hephaestus is smart. He's not dumb because of his limp. He would have crafted a mechanism to hide from Hermes. There is another Olympian who might be able to find him, though."

Aphrodite scoffed. "Who?"

"Hestia," Aries said.

Aphrodite sneered and Eros frowned.

"How would Hestia be able to help?" the youngest god asked.

"She won't. Even if she could," Aphrodite argued. "Hestia has abandoned us. She spends more time in the mortal realm than on Olympus. She has neglected the home and hearth she was tasked to protect."

"Have you forgotten how she helped Demeter raise Persephone? I know you were not around when my siblings and I were young, but Hestia was more of a mother to Athena, Hephaestus, and I than our parents," Ares shot back. "Hestia knows Hephaestus. Probably better than anyone else. At the very least, she and he share an element. She might be able to use her fire to speak with his."

"You're suggesting we go visit your estranged aunt in hopes that she'll magically know where your dysfunctional brother is? I can't believe you, Ares. This matter needs to be left to Zeus and Hermes," she told him.

"The only thing dysfunctional is this family. Now, I'm going to see my aunt. Whether you come or not is up to you, but I refuse to just sit here and wait for my little brother to be found when I'm probably part of the reason he left. Hephaestus hasn't been to Earth in centuries. He doesn't know what humanity is capable of anymore. He could get hurt."

"He's a god," she replied.

"He's a sensitive soul," Aries said.

"I'm coming with you," Eros interrupted. Both of his parents turned to look at him. Aphrodite wore a mask of betrayal while Ares held out a hand for his son to take.

"I'll appreciate the company," Aries told him.

"Do you know where Hestia is?" Eros asked.

Ares nodded. "Lexington, Missouri. We'll land outside of town and drive in. Be sure to bring your bike."

"Styx!" Aphrodite exclaimed. "Hephaestus is my husband. Neither of you are going anywhere without me."

"You'll hate Lexington," Ares droned. "It's a civil war town."

"Nonsense. I love Missouri. The hills are beautiful there, but I refuse to ride on the back of either of your bikes. We'll take my Porsche."

"You can take the Porsche. I need my space," Ares grunted. "Meet me outside of Lexington. I'll see you there…with my bike,"

Aphrodite rolled her eyes when Ares slammed the door, never minding that the home was his and he'd stormed out like it wasn't. "The children of Zeus are always so dramatic."

"Mom," Eros stated calmly but firmly, "you're the very definition of dramatic."

Chapter Fifteen

Hephaestus and Kiara loaded Zion up in the car and headed to Hestia's home for dinner. After their talk in the guest bedroom, they decided on keeping everything god related a secret from Zion. The boy sat in the back of the car singing along with the radio as Hep drove.

Hestia's house was near the park and the hospital. It was a small home with a porch swing and garden gate. Wildflowers bloomed in vivid colors in their beds and white flowery trees filled the air with a sweet scent.

"Hephaestus," Hestia greeted her guests at the door with a burgundy shawl wrapped around her shoulders. "Kiara. Zion. Thank you for coming. Please come inside, dears. I have gyros cooking."

"What's a gyro?" Zion asked, skipping up the porch steps.

Hestia grinned at him, kneeling so she was at his height. "They're like tacos, but with lamb. You'll enjoy them. Could you do me a favor?"

"Sure!"

"In my backyard there is a playset that hasn't had a child on it in years. Can you go give it some love while I talk to your mom and Hep?"

"Absolutely!" Zion took off through the house to find the back door. Hestia watched him go with a fond look. "He's so energetic," she remarked to Kiara. "You must have your hands full with him."

"He's always up to something," Kiara confirmed. She handed Hestia a bottle of wine. "Thank you for inviting us over... Hestia."

Hestia blinked. She shared a look with her nephew. Taking the wine, she scolded, "Now, Hep. You didn't even wait for your auntie to spill the secret?"

"She figured it out on her own," Hephaestus remarked.

"Does the child know?"

"No," Kiara and Hep stated at the same time.

Hestia nodded. "I see. Well, come inside. I meant what I told

The Fall of Fire

you at the generation center, Hephaestus. We need to talk. Your father..." she glanced around and waved at a woman walking a dog. "Come inside."

The inside of Hestia's home was cozy. It was decorated in deep jewel tones and an array of comfy blankets. A burgundy sofa and matching armchairs sat in front of a fireplace. With a wave of her hand, orange flames blazed to life in the hearth.

When Hestia took a spot in one of the armchairs, Kiara's breath caught. The woman in front of her was no longer an elder but a straight postured, long necked, beauty straight out of a fairy tale. Her red curls were combed over, framing one side of her face while held back by a gold, leafy hair clip.

"Since you know who I am," began Hestia, pouring tea into a China set on the coffee table, "there is no need for me to keep your eyes blind to my true form. Don't worry, if Zion comes inside, he will see a fragile old lady."

She poured Hephaestus and Kiara both a cup of tea and handed it to them. The cup looked comically small in Hephaestus's hand.

"Now, about your father," Hestia locked her too wise eyes on her nephew. "Zeus is livid with you. The titans are waking and Mount Olympus is starting to crumble. If the titans wake up, the reign of the gods is over and the war will decimate the human realm. I applaud you for leaving home and what you are trying to do here in Lexington, Hephaestus, but I must urge you to reconsider."

"I'm not leaving," Hep told her.

"I'm not asking you to leave permanently, but Olympus needs their blacksmith," Hestia said.

"Fuck that!" Hephaestus yelled. He stood, his knees hitting the coffee table, which only served to make him angrier as he sauntered around the sofa. He started to pace. "I can't go back. I won't. The titans are not my problem…"

"They are everyone's problem," Hestia remained calm, even as Hephaestus's behavior set Kiara on edge.

"When you say titans," Kiara began, "do you mean Cronus and Rhea?"

"Those are the strongest, but they are not the ones at large right now," Hestia remarked. "As of the last council meeting, there are two titans that are stirring and one that has fully awoken. Hephaestus helped craft their final prisons. I don't want him to leave you and Zion, but a god cannot neglect their responsibilities. If they do…"

A knock at the door interrupted the trio. Hephaestus stopped his pacing to ask his aunt, "Did you invite someone else?"

"No," Hestia narrowed her eyes at the door and pursed her lips, "but reach out and you'll know as well as I who is on the other side of that door."

Before Hephaestus could do as Hestia asked, the door swung open, and Ares strode in with Aphrodite and Eros behind him.

"Hep!"

If Hephaestus didn't know any better, he would have said that Ares looked relieved to see him. The blacksmith gritted his teeth as his brother dropped his motorcycle helmet on the floor. Ares took a step closer to his brother but was held back by Hestia, who raised a hand and erected an invisible wall in front of him.

"Your boots are muddy," Hestia chided. "Leave them at the door, Ares."

Ares flushed, hurrying to do as his aunt asked.

"You've always been so messy," Hestia remarked. "Come sit. You're right on time for tea."

The Fall of Fire

"You knew they were coming," Hephaestus accused.

Hestia didn't correct him and instead poured tea for her new guests.

"Brother," Ares spread his arms wide in peace, which was a gesture that Hephaestus was sure brought him pain. "I didn't come to fight."

"That would be a first," Hephaestus challenged.

Ares balled his fists at his sides. "I understand how you must have felt, but I've come to return you home. We need you…"

"You need a hammer," Hephaestus spat. "You have no idea how I felt. How I *feel*. You, father's golden child, have always held favor while I get cast aside and ordered to play pageboy. Even my wife, who swore dedication to me, prefers you."

Eros pressed his lips into a tight line, he'd known since he'd come into his powers the truth of his parents' relationship, but he'd never spoken it aloud. It seemed unnecessary since Aphrodite and Ares were public with their affair. Now, though, he wondered if speaking the truth would set his stepfather free. Surely his mom would release Hephaestus from his vows when the truth was revealed.

The god of love shook his head to himself and stepped around the sofa, accepting a cup of tea from his great-aunt. Ares and Hephaestus continued to bicker while Aphrodite stared at her nails in a bored manner.

"Hey," Eros greeted Kiara. "I'm Eros. Sorry for the front seat in my family's drama. We're not the most welcoming lot. Are you a friend of Hestia?"

"I'm Kiara," Kiara introduced herself, holding out a hand for Eros to shake. "A friend of Hep's."

The way Eros took her hand was casual, but a jolt of electricity shot up his arm when their hands connected. His eyes developed a pinkish hue and he quickly let go of her hand.

"Ow," she flexed her fingers. "Did you just shock me?"

The gods froze. Instantly all their attention was on Kiara. Hephaestus swooped down upon her like an overprotective hawk, kneeling next to her to check her hand.

"What did you do?" he seethed at Eros.

"It wasn't me. It was her," Eros stated. "Or rather her love… for…" He tilted his head in a way that made him look like a puppy. "For you."

"What?!" Aphrodite gasped. The goddess of beauty's eyes grew cold, and she turned all their fury upon Kiara. "You tramp!" she spat. "Hephaestus is a married man, yet you lay claim to him?"

Kiara snorted. Mythology said she should be more afraid of Aphrodite but all she felt was annoyance. "Like you're one to talk. You've been banging his brother for eons."

"Why you little…" Aphrodite yelled.

Hephaestus pulled Kiara to her feet and behind him, effectively placing himself between his wife and the mortal woman he'd come to love. "Aphrodite, enough!"

"You dare to order me, husband?" Aphrodite asked.

"Woman," Ares growled, shoving himself between his brother and lover, "stand down." With red-brown eyes, Ares turned his attention to his son. "Eros, what the fuck is going on?"

Hestia hummed, sipping her tea with the smile of someone who was enjoying their favorite soap opera.

Eros shoved up his left sleeve, revealing a glowing arrow on his wrist. "She's found a soulmate."

The youngest god exposed the plain black arrow tattooed on his right wrist. Outside of the left one glowing gold, the arrows were identical. He took Kiara's hand in his left one and the corresponding arrow glowed brighter.

"Can I?" he asked, holding his right hand out for Hephaestus to take. Cautiously, the bushy haired god took his stepson's hand. As soon as his callused fingers met Eros's skin, the right arrow blazed to life.

Eros erupted in joy. A pinkish glow engulfed his entire body, and his dimpled grin grew wider than it ever had. "This is wonderful!" he exclaimed. "Hephaestus, Kiara, you're soulmates."

Aphrodite gasped. Hestia clapped her hands together in delight and a weight fell off Ares's shoulders.

"Brother," Ares clasped Hephaestus's shoulder, pulling him into a tight hug. "This is wonderful news!"

Kiara's hold on Hephaestus tightened, trying to tug him away from Ares, but Hephaestus's gaze locked with Aphrodite and his wife looked on the verge of tears. With a sharp pivot, the goddess of beauty turned on her heel and stormed out of the house.

"Excuse me," Hephaestus stated, releasing himself from both Ares and Kiara. "I'll be right back."

Aphrodite slammed the door behind her, but Hephaestus was quick to follow. As it opened again a ceramic pot near the door exploded. He cursed as shards of the planter struck him.

"Dite," he tried to say in his calmest voice.

She collapsed on the steps, crying into her hands.

"Dite." He took a seat beside her, pulling her into a side hug. "Why are you upset? I'd think this would make you happy."

"I am happy," she sobbed, looking up at him with the most tender expression. "Oh Hephaestus, I'm happier than I've ever been. I…I just wish it hadn't taken so long for you to find her. The years we spent at each other's throats because we knew we didn't belong together. Styx, we used to be best friends before I fell for Ares, and you asked your father for my hand. I never understood why you did it. You knew I didn't love you like I love your brother."

Hephaestus sighed. "I was scared. I didn't want to lose our friendship because you were married to Ares. I acted rashly and selfishly when I requested your hand. I never thought you'd grow to hate me as much as you have."

"I don't hate you. I've always loved you, but I do resent what you did and now..." her laugh was watery, "Now Eros has spoken, and you can truly be happy."

"She's mortal. Staying with her would mean leaving Olympus. Didn't you and Ares come to drag me back?"

"Olympus needs your help, but love is the greatest cause of all. You can't let it go. You could return with us, help us stop the titans, and then return to Kiara and live out the rest of her life with her."

"You're not understanding. I won't just stay with her until she dies. I'll give up my immortality."

Aphrodite leaned back, resting her elbows on the porch. "I would be expecting nothing less from you. Everything you do, you do with the passion of fire. It's all or nothing. Zeus will not be pleased but you have my support and..." she took another steadying breath. With a wide smile, she took his hands in her own, looked into his eyes and stated, "I release you from your vows."

Hephaestus nearly wept. "Dite," her name was like a prayer falling from his lips. So soft, so gentle, like a feather. "I release you from yours. I never should have insisted you said them."

The creaking of a gate stole their attention. Zion ran around the house, swinging a stick like a sword. He paused when he saw Hephaestus and Aphrodite sitting on the porch steps.

"What'cha fighting?" Hep asked.

"Lions," Zion stated. He pointed his stick at Aphrodite and asked, "Who's she?"

"This is…"

"I'm his friend," Aphrodite interrupted. "You can call me Dite. What might your name be?"

"Zion."

"That's a wonderful name. You look a lot like Kiara. Are you her son?"

Zion nodded. "She's my mom…and Hep's my friend too."

"He's the best friend anyone could have," Aphrodite agreed.

Chapter Sixteen

Aphrodite kept her word and she and Ares supported Hephaestus when he announced to the Olympian council that he would be forfeiting his immortality after securing the titans. As expected, Zeus was livid. The king of the gods threatened to throw his son from the Mount, again, but his words were empty. Ares could see through his father's disguise and knew the white-haired man was feeling betrayed. Ares couldn't bring himself to comfort his parents, however, for Hephaestus had been betrayed by them repeatedly in the past. He was excited to see his brother breaking free and promised that he and Aphrodite would visit him and Kiara often. Hestia insisted they stop by her home as well. He thought she was secretly delighted to have more family closer to her and away from the drama of Mount Olympus. She probably hoped that Ares and Aphrodite would eventually forsake their thrones, as well.

With Hephaestus's help, the titans were secured quickly. He,

Ares, and Athena worked side by side to restore and reinforce all of the titans' final resting places and tracked down Pallus to contain him. Pallus, of course, put up quite the fight which took Ares' sword, Athena's spear, and Hephaestus's hammer to put an end to.

While fighting alongside his siblings, Hephaestus sent cyclops in disguise to Kiara's home. Under the guidance of Eros, who formed a fast bond with Zion and Kiara, they repaired Battle Bed and Breakfast. Eros was happy to report to his stepfather that the home passed inspection and that Kiara was eagerly awaiting his return.

The battle lasted only a few days in the realm of gods but was months in the human world. When Hephaestus finally locked up his forge for good, passing on the life coal of the forge to his head cyclops, it was late summer in Lexington. He'd missed most of Zion's summer break and knew just how to make it up to the kid.

Hep pulled up to Battle Bed and Breakfast with his new documents -provided by Hestia – in the glove compartment of the SUV that Ares convinced him to get. He blasted the horn and jumped out of the car. Kiara and Zion opened the door of the bed and breakfast.

"Hep!" Zion ran to the man, who scooped him up into a hug. "You're back!"

"I'm back," Hep grinned, ruffling the boy's hair. "And I brought a gift."

"You did? What is it?" Zion asked.

"We're going on a road trip across the state. Let's go camping!"

"Yes!" Zion fist pumped. "Mom, did you hear?"

"I heard," Kiara stated fondly. "Why don't you go pack. Then we can head out."

The Fall of Fire

"Yippie!" Zion yells in joy.

When Zion ran inside, Kiara fell into Hep's arms. He tilted her chin and kissed her tenderly.

"Hello, my love," he greeted.

"I'm so glad you're here," She snuggled into him. "I was worried about you."

"Ares and Athena had my back. The titans are contained and now we can start the rest of our lives."

She kissed him. "I can't wait."

About the Author:

W.A. Ashes is a Nebraskan author who specializes in young adult fantasy. She published her first work, a short story titled, *The Summer of 1956*, in July 2016 and her debut novel, *White Lies*, in January 2018. She currently resides in Gothenburg Nebraska, where she's surrounded by hay fields, good people, cats, and is constantly in awe of the world around her.

If you enjoyed this book, please consider leaving a review on Amazon or Goodreads. Reviews are important to independent authors as they help their books be seen by a wider audience.

Other Works by W.A. Ashes:

New Adult Urban Fantasy
-White Lies, Web of Lies #1
-Truth Be Told, Web of Lies #2
-What Comes Around, Web of Lies #3

New Adult Clean Romance:

Reigning on Earth

-Mistletoe Mishap, Holiday Romances #1
-The Daily Dead, Holiday Romances #2 (Coming Soon)
-The Strange and Unusual History of Eden Estates

Young Adult High Fantasy
-The Jewel of the Wasted Glades, Tales of Morzania #1
-The Apothecary's Apprentice, Tales of Morzania #2
-The Secrets of Sera's Point, Tales of Morzania #3
-The Spider's Web, Tales of Morzania #4 (Coming Soon)

Juvenile Fantasy
-The Inker, Legends of Room 334 #1
-The Wordsmith, Legends of Room 334 #2
-The Seer, Legends of Room 334 #3 (Coming Soon)

Horror
-All Fun and Games (Icy Fingers Anthology)
-Haunted Hollows: A Collection of Halloween Tales for Young Ghouls and Ghosts

Nonfiction
-Musings: A Collection of Writings
-In the Beginning: An Anxious Author's Guide, Vol 1
-The God Concept: An Anxious Author's Guide, Vol 2
(Releasing in 2024)

The Legend of the Phoenix

~~~~~~~

By: Cassandra Joy
Triggers

Male on Male on Male; Explicit Sex; Possible destruction

Chapter One

Itzamna and Ix Chel were at it again. Coming together in such a spectacular way that the sky and water both shook with their joining. And Kukulkan just wanted… quiet.

Was that really too much to ask? To not have all of creation shaking while the father and mother gods went at it? Seriously. Did sex have to be quite so earth shattering?

Okay, so maybe Kukulkan was just a tad jealous. He wasn't a bad looking dude. Surely he could find someone that would love a lonely serpent god. Right?

With a sigh, he pulled himself up from the lounge he'd been resting on and went on a little walk. Maybe if he got away from this thundering orgy he could clear his mind a little. Lift his mood. Find joy instead of wanting to cut a bitch and her godly consort.

Between one thought and the next, Kukulkan landed on a trail up the side of a mountain in the jungle. Not far above him, vents in the side of the rock were letting off steam. Oh, good. Maybe he'd made it just in time for an epic volcano eruption. That would be a nice break from the boring sameness he'd been enduring lately.

He tried humming a jaunty tune as he began to climb up the trail, basking in the feel of a beautiful and quiet day

Or, quieter, at least from the norm. No jungle was ever truly silent, and this one was no exception. But the soft sounds of trees growing and small animals scurrying through the brush and birds chatting were definitely better than the sex-a-thon going on up above.

Ku kept up the steady climb, but he was so lost in his thoughts and the occasional glimpse of a view out over the jungle that he didn't notice the silent shadow. It wasn't until he paused to drink from a clear spring that he felt the presence.

Kukulkan slowly stood and casually glanced around like he was still unaware. There, behind the cacao tree was a slim figure. Ku smiled softly and continued his climb, but this time, his senses were tuned in.

The more he climbed and felt his stalker, the happier he grew. The man was definitely a hunter. Someone stealthy, healthy, and maybe wealthy? Eh. Who cared if he was wealthy? Ku had more than enough wealth for both of them. Now, if only his hunter would catch him...

* * *

The Legend of the Phoenix

Cho had been on the hunt for days now. Not returning to his village, though it was nearby. Because the jaguar that had been stealing the people's chickens and goats seemed to be circling the village. It did not matter how many times Cho had gotten close this week, it always seemed to disappear right when Cho was ready to pounce.

He needed to kill the beast. But maybe in an hour or two. For now, he needed a rest. And that was when he saw him. The large man walking up the mountain.

He was unlike anyone Cho had ever seen or known. His golden skin was just that: golden. Not a tan color from the sun's attentions, but rather the rich gold of a vein of precious metal. His hair was not black like coal, but rather like onyx.

And he moved so... sensuously. Cho's body had definitely taken note of his broad shoulders, trim hips, and the grace he had. His long, slender hands and his deep voice as he hummed. Oh, yes. Cho's body had woken up.

It had been so long since he'd desired someone. Not since his precious Abha had gone to live with the gods. She had been the brightest part of his life, but she was no more. Her descent into the Underworld had marked the beginning of his ten year celibacy.

Not that it had been intentional. At least, at first. He just missed her so much. But as the years went on and no one caught his eye, he did not bother responding to the many men and women who had pursued him since then. Because why settle for someone he did not want when he was the greatest hunter his people had ever known?

He was likely the greatest hunter simply because he had no wife nagging him to come home every night. Not that he would ever admit that to all of the young boys who said they wanted to

Reigning on Earth

be as great as Cho some day. No use instigating lower birth rates for the next generation just because he did not have someone.

But as the golden man bent over a fallen log to inspect something just off the trail, Cho's body screamed at him. There was no reason to not have someone. Because that ass definitely needed to be his. He had not seen an ass that perfect in so, so long.

"Are you going to drool over my hide all day," the sexy, deep voice said, "or will you do something to actually catch it?"

Cho looked up, startled out of his delicious dream of feasting on the haunch before him. A grinning face was looking over the shoulder attached to the ass, and a blush crept up Cho's face when he realized he had been caught. The greatest hunter his people had ever known. Caught by his prey. Great. Maybe he would not mention this to the others in the village.

"Do you think the hide's owner might want a comfortable place to stay tonight?" Cho asked with a bit of a smirk. God, what was wrong with him? It had been too long since he had flirted.

"That depends," the man turned around and smirked right back at Cho. "By comfortable, do you mean 'in your bed' or just 'in a bed'?"

Cho grinned broadly and slowly looked the man up and down, lingering on his tented loincloth. He appeared to be long and broad all over. Perfect. "That depends," Cho threw back, "on which you prefer."

"Oh, definitely in your bed," the man smiled.

"Then that is what you shall have," Cho nodded. "After you fetch some water while I hunt dinner."

The man paused and tilted his head to the side, considering Cho. His eyes narrowed, and he almost looked like a giant

The Legend of the Phoenix

snake for a moment before that image flew from Cho's head. "You must… fetch water?"

"Only if you want to drink," Cho shrugged. "Come, we have climbed high enough for today. Time to return to the valley."

He turned and began descending the mountain. It was several moments before he realized the man had not followed him. He paused, looking back up the path. The twist in the trail hid where they had been standing before so that Cho could no longer see him. "Come or not! Your choice!" he yelled. He waited for a little while, but when there was no movement above him, he turned to continue on his way home.

As delicious as the golden man looked, he probably was no good for Cho's health. Or concentration. It was probably best if the man did not follow Cho home.

* * *

Kukulkan blinked at the slim man as he walked away. Did he just command a god? The little shit. Ku crossed his arms and glared at the human's back. This was unacceptable. He would make him kneel. Like all should bow before Kukulkan, the Plumed Serpent.

He spun on his heel and continued climbing, grumbling under his breath at how stupid humans were. As he crested another shelf on the side of the mountain, a vent expelled a large billow of smoke. Ku paused to breathe it in, enjoying the heat of the volcano so near rupture. He couldn't wait to see the little man destroyed.

He found himself a rock to perch on and watch the coming destruction.

"Care to share?" A deep voice sounded behind him.

Ku stiffened, in more ways than one, but he hadn't been startled. He gave a disinterested shrug and continued to gaze down into the valley. He didn't bother to move over on the rock at all. If Chaac wanted to sit next to him, he'd do so whether or not Ku shifted to one side.

Chaac sat so that his thigh pressed up against Ku's, and he leaned into Ku a little bit. "Why are you scowling?"

"I'm not scowling," Ku scowled. Damnit. Of course he was. He crossed his arms again and tried to put the mocha skinned man out of his mind. After all, why partake in a sweet little morsel like that when Chaac was next to him? He turned and leaned his forehead against Chaac's. "Why are you here?"

"Escaping Ix Chel and Itzamna, of course," Chaac rolled his eyes, and he pressed back into Ku. "I've been watching this mountain for a while. I figured today was as good a day as any for it to erupt."

Ku laughed and turned back to gaze over the valley again. "A human gave me a command," he whispered.

Chaac's gasp of shock seemed to echo across the valley and bounce back to Ku's ears. "Did he not realize who you are?"

"Apparently not," Ku shrugged again. This time, the disinterest was only feigned, not real. "I'm afraid we've been away from earth too long. The people have forgotten us."

Chaac considered him for a moment before nodding slowly. "How would you like to correct that?"

"With fire," Ku said. He turned to watch one of the nearby vents belch another cloud of smoke.

"I love the way you think," Chaac grinned.

Chapter Two

Cho was not sure why his brain would not let go of the idea of the golden skinned man. He kept forcing it onto other subjects, and his brain kept racing back to the shiny hair, the thick thighs, the strong hands. He needed to let it go. Obviously the man had not been interested enough. And that was the worst part. For too long he had been too good for everyone around him, and now he was not good enough for the one person that stirred his cock.

He made a stop at the stream to fill his waterskin and kept an ear out for anything to hunt for dinner. He knew there was a patch of greens up ahead that were delicious when rubbed into the skin of a peccary. It was one of his favorite meals.

As he looked for a peccary squadron, he felt the ground rumble. What were the gods doing now? He looked up the side of the mountain, and his eyes widened in panic. The mountain was smoking. And not a bit of steam from one hole or another. No, this was clouds and clouds of dark ash.

Cho turned to run down the side of the mountain to his village. He had to warn them. Something was very wrong and he did not want his people to be hurt. But then he paused. He looked back up the side of the mountain and winced. He could not let the golden skinned man be hurt either.

With a sigh, Cho ran up the trail. He pushed all of his strength into his legs, and he climbed faster than he ever had before. But when he crested a ledge halfway up the mountain, he slid to a stop and stared in awe.

The man with the broad shoulders stood next to one with even wider shoulders. The new companion also had onyx hair that fell to his waist. His hips weren't as slim as the first man's, but his thighs and biceps had to be twice as large. He was a stunning example of masculinity.

The two of them stood shoulder to shoulder, facing away

from Cho, looking up at the top of the mountain. They each had an arm raised, and they were chanting some song. It seemed like they were commanding the mountain to quake. Commanding it to rain fire. Commanding it to… kill all of Cho's people.

Before he could really think about it, he was screaming at them, running to push against their backs and curse them. "Do not kill my people!" he cried.

The two turned in eerie silence just as Cho reached them. They stood and let him grasp their arms, not moving a muscle. Cho continued to cling to them. "I will not let you harm the K'iche'! Take me. Punish me for all my crimes. But do not hurt my people!"

"Why do you think we punish the people?" the broader one asked.

Cho took a deep breath, then fell to the ground before them. "I did not respect you for who you are." He held himself stiffly. He could see so clearly now what he had missed before. The sight of the second one had opened his eyes. "You are the gods, and I did not bow as I should have before. Please, punish me, but not my people."

And then he waited. He stared at the ground underneath his face, kept his shoulders still, silently begged them with all of his heart to grant his people mercy.

"What is your name, human?" The voice came so suddenly after long moments of silence that Cho nearly lept out of his skin.

"Ch-Cho," he choked out. "My lord."

"Cho, rise," it was the first one again, the one he had flirted with. Cho slowly stood and dared to raise his eyes to their knees. But he could not manage to look at their faces.

The Legend of the Phoenix

* * *

Chaac looked down on this human that Kukulkan had become obsessed with. Sure, Ku had tried to hide it from Chaac, but that was pointless since no one knew him better. Before the command, this little human had had Ku wrapped around his finger. And looking at him now, Chaac could see why.

His eyes were a soft brown that reminded Chaac of milky chocolate and lazy nights feasting on Ku. His hair was a wiry black that he kept held back in a band that Chaac's fingers itched to pull free. His spine was oh so straight as he stood before them.

"The mountain needs to erupt, Cho," Ku said softly. "It matters not what you or your people have done. It's time for the mountain to burn."

Chaac raised an eyebrow at Ku, but didn't contradict him in front of the human. He'd been eager to wipe out the people just moments ago because Cho had forgotten them. Now he said Cho's words didn't matter simply because Cho prostrated himself before Ku? Chaac filed that away in his memory for future use: Kneel before Ku with pretty words to get anything I want from him.

"Why should we save your people when the mountain must be released of its pressure?" Chaac asked aloud.

"They have done nothing wrong, my lord," Cho begged. "I am the one that deserved your wrath. Take me. Do with me as you wish. But please spare my people."

Chaac exchanged a glance with Ku. It was a generous offer. Could Ku really ignore the slight?

"You are willing to give up your life for the people?" Ku clarified.

"Yes, my lord." Cho nodded eagerly. "I will give you anything, including my life."

"Then that is what I shall have," Ku nodded. "You have until the sun rises in the morning to say goodbye and end your life in the village. When the sun breaks the horizon, you will be here, ready to come with us."

"Yes, my lord!" Cho fell to his knees again and kissed both of their feet before scurrying back down the mountain.

Chaac turned to Ku. "We're still going to erupt the mountain, aren't we?"

Ku smirked. "It depends on how good his blow job skills are."

Chaac laughed and pulled Ku toward a nearby cave. "Let me remind you of what he'll have to compete with."

Ku smirked as he gladly followed Chaac, pulling off his loincloth as he walked.

* * *

Cho ran faster than he ever had before. He must get to the village. He must tell his ahaw, the village leader, what had happened. What was to come. When he entered the village, he pulled himself to an abrupt stop and stared.

All of the people were gathered around the ahaw, crying out to him about the mountain's smoke and ash. Fear was thick in the air.

Cho pushed his way through the crowd to the ahaw and whispered into his ear. "Ahaw, I can stop the mountain from exploding. But if I do, I will not be coming back."

The ahaw turned and looked at him. "Did you speak with the gods?"

The Legend of the Phoenix

"Yes, my ahaw," Cho nodded. "I can stop this. Please let me."

"And lose our greatest hunter?" Surely Cho did not hear panic in the village leader's voice? "Lose a leader of the people?"

"Yes, ahaw," Cho looked down. He could not meet the ahaw's eyes. "Let me do this for the people. Let me stop this disaster."

And then the village leader, the ahaw, pulled Cho into his arms. They buried their faces in each other's necks and fought to hold back tears. Cries of pain. A lifetime of love and loss shared in one moment.

"Goodbye, father," Cho whispered as he pulled away. "I will see you in the Underworld."

Then Cho turned from his father, the ahaw. He turned from his village. He turned from his people. And he ran up the mountain. No use taking anything with him when his life was forfeit. He had no need of possessions when he would be dead before sunrise.

Chapter Three

Kukulkan smirked as Chaac came again. He'd been taking great pleasure in reacquainting himself with Chaac's deliciously muscled body.

The rock beneath them was pleasantly warm now that they'd stopped pushing the mountain to erupt. The rumbling had died out and the smoke and ash no longer filled the air. It would still need to explode soon. Just maybe not tonight.

As Chaac sucked Ku's tip into his mouth, a noise came from the cave's entrance. Cho stood there, staring at the two of them with an open mouth and a thickening cock.

"Come," Ku managed to get out right before Chaac nipped his slit, causing Ku's hips to jerk up. "Join us."

Cho tripped forward, falling onto his knees next to Ku. His

eyes scanned over Chaac lying between Ku's thighs, over Ku's arms stretched over his head, over the two gods taking pleasure in each other. Cho unconsciously licked his lips, and Ku grinned.

"Cho," Ku hissed. "You will do exactly as Chaac tells you to do. You will obey him quickly and enthusiastically. And if he is pleased with your work, we just might spare your life."

Chaac slowly pulled off of Ku's painfully hard cock and looked Cho up and down. "Remove your clothing."

Cho quickly jumped up to obey; Ku's mouth watered at what he saw. The little human was simply beautiful. So leanly strong. So delicious. Oh so sexy.

Once Cho stood before them bare–and hard–Chaac nodded. He ran his palm over the tip of Ku's cock again then moved from between his thighs. "You will stand there and not move," Chaac whispered as he stood and moved around Cho, slowly investigating every inch of skin.

Ku rose to his feet and began circling Cho from the other direction. He drug a finger around Cho's waist, making sure not to dip too low. Teasing him.

When Ku and Chaac passed each other behind Cho, Ku made sure to steal a quick kiss before continuing his inspection of the man.

They both ended up back in front of Cho again and simply gazed upon the sexy K'iche'. Cho tried oh so hard to stand still, but his hands and knees were trembling. Ku looked toward Chaac and winked. "I think our little human is ready to be punished for his insult." And what a pleasurable punishment it would be!

"I do believe so," Chaac grinned back. He stepped to the side of Cho and palmed his ass.

Ku stepped to the other side and turned Cho's face to taste his lips. Cho parted his lips on a sigh, and Ku dove in. He relished Cho's soft lips and rough tongue and the feel of Cho's lean body pressed against his.

Chaac pressed in closer from the other side as he wrapped a hand around Cho's cock. A low groan came from Cho, and Ku swallowed it down. As Chaac pulled Cho in a slow rhythm, Ku feasted, nipping and licking away from Cho's mouth and down his jaw and neck. He licked the sweat pooling in the cleft of Cho's throat and moaned at the taste.

He forced himself to pull away and go sit against the cave wall, watching Chaac pleasure Cho. When Cho came all over Chaac's hand, Chaac leaned in to whisper a command. "Go kneel before Kukulkan and swallow him down."

Cho came forward on wobbly legs and sunk to his knees before Ku. Ku spread his legs wide to give him room. Cho reached forward to take Ku in his hand when Chaac said. "No, do not touch him with anything but your mouth. Hands behind your back." Cho quickly obeyed then leaned forward to suck Ku down.

Ku held himself still, wanting to grab Cho and pull him into his lap, but knowing that Chaac had other plans for him. He looked up into Chaac's golden eyes and grit his teeth. Chaac grinned back at him.

Cho ran his tongue up the vein of Ku's cock, and Ku arched up into his mouth at the sensation. He might have thrust a bit hard since Cho began to choke. Before he could pull off, though, Chaac pushed his head further into Ku's lap. "Eat him, Cho. You disrespected him. Commanded a god. You must make up for it. Give Kukulkan all of your pleasure."

So he did. Cho sucked and nipped and swallowed around

Reigning on Earth

Ku's cock over and over again. When Ku came, Cho stayed and did his best to swallow everything Ku gave him.

Ku sat back with a smile and locked eyes with Chaac.

* * *

Chaac was quite pleased with their little human. Ku certainly seemed so. Chaac couldn't take his eyes off of Cho's ass the whole time he'd been blowing Ku, and now Chaac couldn't think of anything better to do than to sink into it.

As Ku leaned back in pleasure, Chaac knelt behind Cho and grabbed his hips. He quickly conjured oil to slick his cock before slowly pushing it into Cho. Cho arched back into Chaac with a pleased cry.

Ku reached up and ran his hands down Cho's chest, tweaking his nipples, running along his ribs. Cho squirmed on Chaac's cock, and Chaac nearly passed out from the pleasure. But he held on because this was exactly what he'd been hoping for when he'd followed Ku down to Earth. He'd needed a diversion; he'd wanted Ku in his arms. Cho and Ku together was even better.

Ku scooted forward so that his legs wrapped around Cho and Chaac's knees. He rutted his quickly hardening cock between Cho's thighs as Cho twisted on Chaac.

The three of them moved together in a dance older than Earth. Older than the Underworld. Yes, this dance came straight from Ōmeyōcān, the highest of heavens. And Chaac and Ku were masters of it.

When Cho was nearing his completion, Chaac reached around to grab the human's cock while Ku leaned forward to swallow his cries. Three of them came together, a writhing,

The Legend of the Phoenix

sweaty, sticky mess of pure satisfaction.

Chaac gently lowered Cho to lie on the ground next to Ku, then he wrapped himself around the little K'iche'. The three of them lay there, breathing deeply and letting their muscles lose their tension.

Chaac was almost asleep when Cho quietly asked, "So what do the gods have in mind for my punishment?"

Ku burst out laughing, and Chaac couldn't help but chuckle with him.

* * *

Honestly, it was not funny. Did these gods not realize that Cho was worried about his people? Did they not know how scary it was to walk away from all you had ever known?

Cho tried to pull away, to remove himself from between their two golden bodies. But they held onto him, keeping him right where they wanted him.

"Was that not punishment enough?" Ku asked softly.

Although Cho had never lain with a male before, he would not have called what they did a punishment. Surely the god was jesting.

"Cho, I hear you're the greatest hunter the K'iche' have ever known," Chaac said as he nuzzled his face into Cho's neck.

"Um, I guess?" Why was the golden god asking about that?

"Was that a question?" Ku asked.

"I am not sure I would say greatest ever." Cho tried to shrug it off, but Ku just held him tighter. "Definitely greatest currently alive."

Chaac and Ku both laughed again.

"You've been having trouble with a jaguar," Chaac noted.

"Terrorizing the people at night and then slinking away before you can hunt him down."

Cho nodded slowly. "I have been tracking him all week. I have never known a foe like this. And I am too far away from axis mundi to call upon… the gods…" Cho swallowed as realization hit him. His prayers had been heard, even though he had not left the village to travel to the great city. The gods had come to Earth themselves to help him. And he had commanded one and cried upon the chests of both. It was a wonder they had not killed him yet.

"We have come," Chaac said seriously. Ku smirked at him, making Chaac roll his eyes at his fellow god. "And we wish to give you a gift to defeat this evil."

Cho sat up, pulling the two of them to sitting positions since they would not let him go. "You will help me kill the jaguar?"

"No," Ku said softly. "We'll make you into a hunter greater than the jaguar. It's up to you to kill him on your own."

Cho pondered for a moment. "What kind of hunter?"

"One never before seen," Ku said. "I will give you my feathers."

"And I will give you my fire," Chaac said. "Together, you will be a fire bird of great strength, agility, and cunning."

"The jaguar will not know how to fight such a beautifully deadly bird," Ku added.

Cho stood and moved to the cave's mouth, looking over the valley of his people. Over the jungle where he had been hunting for days. He already knew he would never go back to the K'iche'. So they would never know that he had become something other than a man. He slowly nodded as his thoughts came to a conclusion. "I will do this." Cho turned to look at the two gods. "For the people."

Chapter Four

Ku leaned into Chaac as the huge firebird flew out of the cave. Cho's transformation had been easy enough to accomplish. After all, Ku and Chaac both had great power. The only question now was whether or not Cho's new form would be enough to battle the jaguar.

"Do you think he'll kill it?" Ku asked.

"Yes," Chaac said as he wrapped an arm around Ku's shoulders. "He is very determined to protect his people."

"Whether it be from a jaguar or a couple of gods," Ku chuckled.

"Yes," Chaac grinned.

"The mountain still needs some relief," Ku pointed out.

"We can direct it to vent into the other valley, away from his people." Chaac shrugged.

"Perhaps, yes," Ku pondered. "Maybe I shouldn't have given him so many of my feathers."

"You can still fly, my beautiful plumed serpent," Chaac cooed into his ear. "And now he can as well."

"Why do I feel as if we've sent our child off to die?"

"Do you not trust the greatest hunter of the K'iche' people to use our gifts to hunt?" Chaac nuzzled the side of Ku's head, lending comfort.

"I do," Ku pulled Chaac's other arm around him so that Ku was surrounded. "It is the jaguar I do not trust. What if he's a demon sent by the death gods?"

"Do not doubt our little phoenix," Chaac said. "He will prove tonight why he is the greatest."

Ku nodded and snuggled closer into Chaac's arms.

* * *

Cho's new firebird eyes spotted the jaguar moments after night had fallen. This was truly amazing. He had been unable to see the creature while under the tree canopy, but now he could see it through the leaves. How odd.

Cho swooped toward the jaguar, withholding his instinct to sound a battle cry. He wanted to surprise the big cat this time.

He came through the branches at an angle behind the jaguar, making sure to stay in his blind spot. Once he got close, he swung his talons forward and grabbed the jaguar's neck.

For a second or two, the jaguar's body lifted off the ground, but then he began to struggle and squirm in Cho's grasp. Once Cho had him a good distance into the air, he let the cat go, hoping he had damaged the spine enough that the jaguar would not be able to land on his feet.

He arced through the air, turning back to make another run at the monster. Now he sounded his battlecry. It was a low screech that was unlike anything Cho had ever heard before, much less had made. It sent a shiver of pleasure down his spine as he swung his claws forward again.

This time, he snatched at the jaguar's face, sinking a talon into its eye. The cat roared in pain and swiped at Cho. But Cho was too quick, too agile now. He spun out of the jaguar's reach and made sure to slice open as much of its face as he could in the process.

Cho spun around again, crying out as he raked his talons across the cat's back. He continued pass after pass. And though the jaguar fought back, Cho rarely gave him time to land any blows. Cho altered his angles of attack each time to surprise the evil monster. He went after its belly, its tail, its neck and face. Over and over Cho attacked.

Until finally, the jaguar lie on the ground, panting as his blood

The Legend of the Phoenix

poured from the thousand talon cuts all over its body.

It was not dead yet, but that was just a technicality. Cho had finally defeated the jaguar, the evil that had been stalking and preying on his people. After weeks of fruitless hunting, he had finally won.

With a victorious cry, Cho soared into the sky. He could not wait to tell his two gods!

Chapter Five

"He did it," Ku said with a note of awe in his voice. "Our little K'iche' slew his jaguar."

"Yes, he did," Chaac said with a smile. "Do you think we should reward him?"

Ku threw back his head and laughed. "Yes, we shall."

Just then, the phoenix landed in front of them. But instead of shifting back into his human form, the bird just squawked at them.

It hopped around, flapping its wings, looking about as upset as a giant fire bird could possibly look.

"Can you not shift?" Chaac asked with concern.

It cawed and crowed and generally continued to cause a commotion.

Ku and Chaac both stepped forward and reached out to stroke the bird's head. When it cooed and nuzzled into Ku's hand, Ku's cock jumped to attention.

Ku managed to rein in his desire enough to push some power into Cho, the avenging firebird.

Suddenly, he burst into brighter, higher, hotter flames. Then a gust of wind came up over the edge of the mountain, and the fire puffed out. Ashes blew away in the wind. And a very naked and shivering Cho stood there.

Reigning on Earth

"Oh, good! You're K'iche' again!" Chaac grinned.

"I am c-c-cold," Cho said.

"I think we can do something about that," Ku said with a grin. He took the man's hand and pulled him back toward their little cave of wonders.

This time, Ku wanted to taste Cho. To devour him. Swallow him whole. Feel his seed filling his mouth.

Once Ku had Cho lying on the ground, he pushed the warrior's knees to his chest and settled himself on the ground before him.

Just as Ku was about to lick a stripe from Cho's balls to his head, Chaac knelt beside Cho and leaned forward to kiss him.

Ku watched in pleasure as the two of them tangled tongues. Eventually he remembered that he'd wanted to taste Cho, so he went ahead and licked him from stem to stern.

And, oh, how wonderfully Cho tasted, like burning coals. Ku sucked the K'iche's cock into his mouth and hummed in pleasure around it.

When he did, Cho arched up with a cry, pulling away from Chaac's questing mouth to scream "more" at Ku. And Ku was more than happy to give it to him.

They stayed there with Chaac and Ku tasting Cho all over his body for what felt like days. But it didn't feel like enough. Ku didn't think he'd ever get enough of the slender man.

After Cho's third–or maybe fifth?–orgasm, Ku and Chaac switched places and began again. They licked and nipped and sucked and bit every inch of Cho's skin until he'd come a few more times.

Until he was a wrung-out, limp mess of come and moans.

He was the most beautiful sight Ku had ever seen.

"How'd you like your reward for defeating the jaguar, little bird?" Chaac whispered into Cho's skin.

The warrior lifted his head and looked down his body at the two gods that had been worshiping him.

"Do you have any other enemies you wish me to defeat?"

Ku's and Chaac's twin grins of evil glee spread over their faces.

"We can find some for you," Ku said. "Anything for you."

Chaac added, "Our avenging phoenix."

The End

About Cassandra

Cassandra Joy is an author of adventure romances. She's an avid reader of most every type of romance, but loves steamy MM action and one woman being pleasured by multiple men the most.

While Cassandra loves fantasizing about just such delicious stories, she's happily married to a single man. He's the father and manager of her brood of crazy offspring. They also have a fat cat that thinks he's a guard dog.

Sign up for Cassandra's newsletter (CassandraJoy.Me) to get notifications about upcoming books. You can find Cassandra at CassandraJoy.us/links.

Also by Cassandra

CJ's Neighborhood

Dawn of a New Day

A Touch of Sunshine

Out of the Fire

Second Chance at Romance

Chaos at PolyTech University (with G.R. Loreweaver)
   Death & Chaos
   Longing & Chaos
   Lust & Chaos
   Trial & Chaos
   Love & Chaos

Ax to the Heart
   Finding His Heart
   Finding His Mage
   Finding His Forever (September 2023)